Sammy & Me

Sammy & Me

Marie Yates

LODESTONE BOOKS

Winchester, UK
Washington, USA

First published by Lodestone Books, 2017
Lodestone Books is an imprint of John Hunt Publishing Ltd., Laurel House, Station Approach,
Alresford, Hants, SO24 9JH, UK
office1@jhpbooks.net
www.johnhuntpublishing.com

For distributor details and how to order please visit the 'Ordering' section on our website.

ISBN: 978 1 78535 502 8
978 1 78535 503 5 (ebook)
Library of Congress Control Number: 2016939769

A CIP catalogue record for this book is available from the British Library.

Design: Stuart Davies

Printed and bound by CPI Group (UK) Ltd, Croydon, CR0 4YY, UK

One

It happened almost like I'd planned. I'd lived it so many times in my head that results day shouldn't have been big deal. It really was a big deal. I hardly slept last night and this morning I was so nervous I couldn't eat breakfast. That's a pretty big sign that something isn't right. My hungry hound, Reggie was pleased as he enjoyed my slice of toast. He didn't care that it was results day; nothing gets in the way of his morning walk and today was no exception.

We were in the park earlier than usual and playing with every stick he could find meant that I had a happy distraction for an hour or so. Even though he's a big dog, he is just as happy lying down with his stick as he is running around with it in his mouth. It keeps me occupied too, as trying to distract him with his other toys so that he doesn't hurt himself is a constant work in progress. We got home and it still wasn't even nearly time to leave. I was due to meet Maya, Callie and Katie at school and Mum had taken the day off work to drive me there. She was more nervous than I was this morning, and we were going to have a nice big breakfast but neither of us could face it. Mum had planned the whole day, it didn't matter what the results were, we were going out for a celebratory lunch and intended to have a good time together. Can't beat some enforced fun! I don't think Mum expected much from my results. She has never said it aloud, but I think she's just pleased I stayed in school and didn't have a total meltdown. Anything else is a bonus.

We drove to school in silence. Mum was nervously tapping the steering wheel in time to the music on the radio, and it was frustrating me. It could have been worse, at least she wasn't singing. Thankfully, Maya and Callie were waiting at the school gates, and as we got there, Katie and her Mum pulled up behind us in their car. 'I love you and I'm really proud of you,' was the last thing I heard as I slammed the car door and joined my friends to learn our fate.

When I had thought about this day, I couldn't imagine opening the envelope. In my head, I would take it back to car and open it with Mum. In reality, I couldn't open the envelope quickly enough and the four of us gathered in the corner of the sports hall to scream letters at each other.

'I GOT A C IN MATHS,' I screamed at the girls who'd joined me.

They all looked at me and went very quiet as Katie gently said, 'Don't worry, Dani, we'll help with your re-takes, it'll be okay.'

'No, no, no…you don't understand. I never have to do maths again. I got a 'C'! I got six As and three Bs too. But I can't believe I got a 'C' in maths.'

The relief showed immediately on their faces as they started screaming out their own letters. We'd all done well, especially Katie who had managed to get mostly A*s.

I was so excited for her as she worked really hard. We all did, but Katie had big dreams and this was a pretty clear sign that she was going to make them happen.

We calmed down and started to walk back to where Mum and Jenny, Katie's mum, were impatiently waiting. They told me to do the same thing to Mum as I'd done to them and just tell her about the 'C' in maths. While Jenny burst into tears at the sight of all those A*s and Katie seized the opportunity to ask for a new phone, I excitedly told Mum that I'd got my 'C'.

Without missing a beat, she hugged me and said, 'That's brilliant, darling, I know how much you hate maths and now you never have to do it again. So, what about all the subjects you do like?'

I handed over my results. She cried. She wasn't as hysterical as Katie's mum who by this point had agreed to the new phone and a party, but she was obviously pleased.

Above everything else, I felt relief. I had won. This time last year I was a wreck. I was terrified about starting the new school and I was concentrating on being able to call myself a survivor, not a victim. Things didn't get any better when I started school. If someone had told me that after surviving rape I would be faced with a year of torture at the hands of school bullies, I wouldn't have got out of bed.

I'd passed all of my exams. I walked into school with my head held high surrounded by my new friends and didn't give the bullies a second thought. It wasn't until Mum and I were sitting having lunch that she asked, 'Have you seen any of the bullies lately?'

'No, I didn't see any of them,' I replied. 'I didn't even think to look.'

In fact I'd been too busy concentrating on what mattered to me, and more than anything, I was hoping that I would never, ever, be forced to do maths again. It's funny, even though I'm really pleased with my results, it's the 'C' that has made me happiest of all. I have choices now. I need to decide about 6th Form and which subjects I want to do but thinking about it hurts my head.

I have taken Mum's advice this evening and curled up on the sofa to watch a film. I have Reggie with me but he doesn't want a cuddle as he's a little bit distracted by the biscuits Mum bought me!

She couldn't let me watch the film in peace though and just as it was getting exciting, Mum reached for a tissue. With leaking eyes and a breaking voice I heard her say, 'Today's been a good day. I'm proud of you. After everything that's happened, today has proven that surviving is all about willpower. Even though there've been loads of times that I'm sure you wanted to give up, it's been worth all the hard work.' She patted my hand.

'Yeah, I know, now shush and let me watch the film.'

Two

Happy Birthday to me! I feel like celebrating this year. My birthday was a real non-event last year with everything else that was going on. I couldn't concentrate on anything other than getting away from the place where I had been raped, away from all my friends who couldn't stop treading on eggshells around me and just starting again. When I look back at last summer I can't believe how different I was. If it wasn't for Reggie and starting taekwondo I'd probably be a complete mess now. If I let myself think about it for too long it all gets a bit scary. Today, once I get my arse out of bed, I'm going to celebrate. Mum said she'd take Reggie for his morning walk so that I can have a lie in and then she's bringing me breakfast in bed. I haven't heard them come back in yet so I'm just lying in bed, writing. Not a bad start to the day.

Being one of the youngest in my year really sucks, because now that it's the summer holidays, everyone else has enjoyed their sixteenth and they're counting down the days to their first driving lesson. They don't really care that it's my birthday. I checked my phone and had 'Happy Birthday' messages on Facebook. I'm not sure that really counts though because if it wasn't for the Facebook update most of those people wouldn't even know it was my birthday. I know that I have cards from a couple of my old friends, which is nice, and even though Maya, Callie and Katie are all away, they dropped off presents and cards before they left. Mum has talked about us going on holiday but I only want to go somewhere where Reggie can come too so that has cut our options right down! She said that we could go and spend some time catching up with people where we used to live but the look on my face told her how I felt about that idea. She hasn't mentioned it again. So, today I have a visit from my grand-parents to get excited about. Lucky me!

'Daniiiiiiiii.'

I can smell bacon! Laters!

... Another birthday over and although it wasn't nearly as bad as last year, it was a bit of non-event again. It was nice to get messages from people and when I read my cards, I felt a tiny bit tempted to agree to visit our old friends. It didn't last long. I knew, in reality, it would just be awkward.

'How's Reggie?' was the first question out of Grandpa's mouth.

Grandma rolled her eyes and shouted, 'Happy Birthday, darling.'

'Yeah, thanks!' As usual, the visit had started with pointless discussions.

'The traffic was awful on the motorway and we had patches of drizzle in places,' was Grandpa's best attempt at small talk.

I wanted to shout 'who cares?', but managed to stop myself.

'Stop talking about the weather and congratulate Dani on her results before you start playing with the dog,' Grandma chipped in. But their only real focus was Reggie. I'm pretty sure he's the only reason they came to visit.

We got rid of them after lunch but not before they'd spent at least an hour with Reggie in the garden. Mum and I were just sitting in the kitchen watching and they didn't seem to notice. It was nice that they weren't going on and on about how sad I must be, which is what they usually do, but I was still relieved when they'd gone.

Mum sighed as she shut the door behind them. 'We should be able to get to Christmas without another visit now.'

'Let's hope so.'

We went back into the kitchen to find Reggie sound asleep in his bed. At least he'd enjoyed the visit! Mum disappeared into the cupboard under the stairs and came out with another present for me. That was a surprise as I'd already had so much. Money, clothes, iTunes vouchers and an amazing new phone. The really annoying thing about getting a new phone was that all I wanted to do was set it up but I had to leave it to charge before I could. Anyway, it was a big square present and before I could rip it open I had to listen to Mum's little speech.

'I'm so proud of you and how you've turned everything around in the last year. I know that it really hasn't been easy but today's a turning point for you. You've passed your exams, you have your whole future ahead of you and you can be anything you want to be,' she gushed. 'I'm one hundred per cent behind you and I hope this present inspires you as you start the next chapter in your life.'

As Mum's eyes looked as though they were about to leak. I ripped open the present to find the most amazing picture I had ever seen. It was a silhouette of a girl on a beautiful beach at sunset doing a perfect taekwondo kick. It's now hanging up on the wall in my bedroom so it's the first thing I'll see when I wake up. One day, that will be me. I've only been doing taekwondo for a year but my big goal is still to get my black belt.

As soon I put the picture up on my wall I had the urge to practice as I have another grading coming up soon. I then wished I hadn't eaten quite so much at lunch time.

There hasn't been a big party or loads of friends to spend the day with but it definitely hasn't been the worst birthday I've ever had. I now have a whole year before I can start looking forward to my first driving lesson, and there's that small issue of figuring out what I'm going to do next. Mum's been really good about letting me wait for the results and then enjoying my birthday, but I know she won't be able to keep quiet about it for much longer.

Three

Yeah, I spoke too soon. The first words out of Mum's mouth this morning were, 'It's the middle of August now, Dani, so it's time to start looking to the future and making some decisions.'

I tried not to roll my eyes as I replied, 'I know, Mum, I've decided I definitely want tea and I'll have cereal when I'm back from walking Reggie.'

Apparently, I'm not funny.

I thought that I might have a bit of time before having to answer a whole load of questions about my future, but when I got home from walking Reggie, Jane was already sitting in the kitchen with her notebook.

Jane, Mum's best friend, was staying for a couple of days. The official reason was that she wanted to catch up with us both and enjoy some time walking the dog (she tolerates Reggie, at best). We all knew that she was going to use her skills as a psychologist to make sure that by the time she left to go home, I had the next year or so mapped out and a good idea of what I wanted to do in the future.

'Do I at least get to open my birthday present before you start trying to work your mind magic on me,' I said, before she had a chance to start on me.

'Happy Birthday,' she shrieked. 'And I'm going to ignore that comment for now.'

Before the court case, Jane bought me a lovely bracelet with two charms that she had chosen. One is the letter 'B' which stands for the fact she believes in me 100 per cent and the other has red hearts on it, which is supposed to remind me that I'm loved, and red is the colour that represents courage.

I looked at the new charms. 'Amazing! Thank you, thank you, thank you. These charms are perfect. I love them, but is that a Labrador?'

Jane grabbed it out of my hand and held it up in the air. 'It looks like Reggie to me.'

'Jane, it's a Labrador but in your world, I guess that's a pretty good likeness, even though Reggie is half Rottweiler and half German Shepherd.'

'It's a dog, it could have been worse as I nearly bought the cat charm.'

The other one is a pretty, green-coloured charm that represents optimism. As I opened it, Jane said, 'With the strength you've shown this last year, there's every reason to be optimistic about what the future holds.'

Cue the speech about the future as she moves on from confusing Reggie with a Labrador.

There was a letter addressed to me that was sitting by my cuppa. As Jane was wittering on about the importance of focusing on what I wanted for my future and making sure I had thought about the subjects I wanted to study, I opened my post. It was like the universe was laughing at me. The letter was from the Sixth Form College I had applied to saying that I needed to make my final subject choices and they had included all the details about enrolment.

'I don't know what I want to do. I don't even know if I want to go to Sixth Form,' I said. Jane looked like I had told her I was going to run away to the circus. 'But as I'm not ready for the Olympic Taekwondo Team just yet, I can't figure out an alternative.' I paused. 'I know that I need to decide and I definitely want to do something productive…I'm just not sure what. I like the idea of starting Sixth Form. It's supposed to be a lot more relaxed than school and anything will be better than that place.'

I didn't tell Jane, but I'm a bit nervous that I might see some of the bullies there. At least at Sixth Form, we're all new so I won't be different to anyone else. Starting Year Eleven as the new kid definitely didn't help me last year and I might have simply been unlucky…story of my life. I'm not focusing on that though.

'I know that Katie and Maya are definitely going to this Sixth Form so it's brilliant I'll have people to go to enrolment with,' I ventured. 'Callie is going off to some fancy art college. She's so good at art and she's desperate to get an apprenticeship and become a world famous tattoo artist. I said that she could tattoo me when she's really good at it.'

It made me laugh that Jane was less worried about that than they idea of me not going to Sixth Form at all.

'I won't mention that to your mother as I don't think any of you want her to practice on your skin just yet! I hope you'll keep in touch with her, she sounds like fun.'

'I hope we keep in touch too. I'll make more of an effort with her than I did with my old friends.'

Katie will probably do a million A Levels and she'll pass every single one with flying colours. I bet she's having the exact same conversations with her mum as I've been having with Jane. The only difference is that while I was convinced I wanted to be a psychologist, I'm not so sure now. For Katie, she wants to be everything and can't decide. In the last month, she has wanted to be a vet, a doctor, a lawyer and an architect. The thing is, no matter what she does, she'll be brilliant at it.

Maya is going to study music and a couple of other subjects she enjoys. She was going to go to art college with Callie but has now decided that all she really wants to do is music. She has no idea what she wants to do in the future, other than it has to involve music!

Jane snapped me out of thinking about my friends by asking, 'What's your gut telling you?'

I thought for a moment. 'I know I want to make a difference and I know that I want to do something that matters to me. I'm just not sure what matters to me enough to want to study it for another two years. Maybe I should stick to psychology as I can't think of anything else I'd like to do.'

'I'll try not to be offended by that. What about something

with animals considering how much you love that Labrador?

'At least you make yourself laugh, Jane. My maths definitely isn't good enough to be a vet so I'd be getting all the doses of medicine wrong. It's not like I could whip out my phone in the middle of an operation to work out the sums. And I'd be crying all day if I had to put animals to sleep and would probably end up bringing all the stray animals home with me.' I gave her a rueful smile. 'Even though I love that Labrador, I don't think I want to make a career out of it.' So, I'm back to not knowing what subjects to take or what I want to do in the future. Brilliant.

Four

I managed to escape last night while Mum and Jane were cracking open their second bottle of wine. Their ideas about career choices for me were getting silly so I sneaked out as I heard, 'She'd be great on a cruise ship and then we'd get cheap holidays' then 'I know, what if she became the chief taster for a chocolate biscuit company,' followed by a combined shout of 'Freeeeeeee biscuits.' These adults are supposed to be helping me.

Earlier today, Jane asked, 'Are you still using your journal to write about how you're feeling and to write your goals, successes and gratitude lists?'

'Sorry, I've given up on it a bit because I haven't been feeling very motivated.'

Jane rolled her eyes, 'That's exactly when you need to be doing it so that it helps to motivate you.'

'Yeah, yeah, I promise I'll start doing it again.'

I grabbed my bag and ran out to go to taekwondo, hoping that she believed my promise. It felt so good to get some exercise. I'm working towards my green belt, which is tough, but really good fun. I needed it today as I didn't realise how stressed out I was feeling. It wasn't until I left the class that I realised I felt so much better, like a weight had been lifted. It probably had because I trained hard, so should have been lighter in more ways than one.

While I was in the middle of working on my sparring, it came to me. I needed to choose subjects that I enjoy rather than worrying too much about what the future holds.

I have no idea what I want to do for the rest of my life, but I do know that I want it to be something I enjoy. What's the point in trying to talk myself into doing certain subjects just so that I can start working towards a career I'm not sure I want?

This is why I love taekwondo. It's the only place I can think clearly…because I'm not trying to think clearly. It's quite often when I'm focusing on making my body do things I never thought possible that my brain sends me the answers I didn't know I needed. I have been searching for the perfect career rather than thinking about the life I'd like to lead.

Jane asked me yesterday whether I saw myself being in an office, working nine to five, working outside, working with people or animals… 'I DON'T KNOW,' I had helpfully shouted. It all felt so overwhelming. She had a point through; what do I enjoy doing?

I have no idea whether I want to work in an office. It sounds boring but then I also don't think I want to work outside in the winter. I like being around nice people, but I know that you can't always choose the people you have to spend your days with. I love being around Reggie, but I don't know if I want to spend every day with animals. I love taekwondo, but it's not a career choice for me. I've already looked up the entry requirements for psychology degrees and they seem to be pretty chilled about the A level choices as long as you have decent grades. The only way I would stand a chance at getting decent grades is by doing something I enjoy. I hated every second of working for that maths GCSE and the only motivation to pass was the fact I'd never have to do it again. I don't want to spend the next two years feeling like that about the subjects I'm studying.

So, mid-sparring, it came to me: Biology, PE, Psychology and English.

'I've made my decision,' I proudly announced to Mum and Jane, who were still nursing their headaches from last night's wine. 'There're very deep and meaningful reasons for my choices. I love everything I'm learning through taekwondo so Biology and PE should help me to get better. A big part of me is fascinated by what you do, Jane, and what I've learnt about myself over the last couple of years. The way I've recovered has been about changing what's going on in my own head, so understanding more about that through Psychology would be brilliant.' I smiled at them, astonished at my own revelation. 'The decision about English is just as profound – I like reading and writing.'

They were staring at me, as if they couldn't believe I had actually made a decision so I carried on talking.

'There's a college a bit further away that does an 'animal care' course, which looks good but I can care for my own animal at home and am happy with that. That's it. They're my choices. Biology, PE, Psychology and English.'

I didn't think 'because I want to' would be good enough reason, but it was! Yay!

'You're being sensible, Dani, keeping your options open, and they're great choices. I'll help if I can,' said Jane.

Mum admitted, 'I won't be much help but I'll make you tea while you work hard and Reggie will definitely be up for helping with PE practicals.'

After finishing off the last piece of birthday cake, Jane left feeling as if she'd done a great job of helping. I might have burst her bubble by saying, 'It was thanks to escaping the interrogation and going to taekwondo that helped.' I will stick to my promise though and do my goals and stuff.

My goals have changed a bit but I can happily tick off the one that said I'll pass all of my exams in August. Done.

- It is September and I have my green belt in taekwondo
- It is September and I have enrolled in Sixth Form to study Biology, PE, Psychology and English

There's only two but that's good enough for now. My big goal is still black belt and I guess my big A Level goal is to get four As. I suppose I should say A*s but let's not get silly about it.

The main success I've had today is not only choosing my A Level subjects but feeling excited about them. I never thought I'd say that. It must also count as a success that Mum and Jane didn't give me any grief about my choices.

Then there's gratitude. I am so grateful that I had taekwondo to go to today. I'm also grateful for Jane coming to help even though she did do my head in a bit!

Five

It's been a weird day. It was great in loads of ways but then I came home and just felt sad.

I spent the day with the girls and we laughed a lot. I'm so excited that Katie and Maya will be at the same Sixth Form. Callie said she'd miss us all but that she couldn't wait to spend every day drawing and doing loads of arty stuff that I didn't really understand. She said she'd be trying balloon art, which I thought was a joke. It wasn't a joke! She showed us pictures and someone had created the most amazing designs out of balloons. Who knew?! That just goes to show that I have no idea about all the weird and wonderful jobs out there.

The most exciting thing is that we don't have to wear a uniform. It sounds good, in theory, but also gets me a bit worried as I'm all about jeans and hoodies. This doesn't make me the most fashionable of students. Katie always looks like she's just stepped out of the hairdresser and both Maya and Callie are into the latest trends. I couldn't care less and as long as my clothes have pockets for my phone and lip balm I'm happy.

'Don't worry about it,' Callie told me. 'You'll be the coolest student around when I've covered you in tattoos and made you a balloon outfit!'

Yeah, the balloon outfit would be like putting a sign over my head saying 'bully me please'. I think I'll pass on that one. They did make me feel better as I won't be walking into most of the lessons on my own. Maya will be doing English and Psychology with me and Katie is signing up for Biology. That's brilliant, but it leaves PE as the subject that I'm most scared of AND the one I'll be facing on my own.

Thinking about PE has me worried. I'm already considering dropping it, or switching to another subject. I could take a safe option like History and just keep my head down. I have a suspicion though that History really is as boring as it sounds. After the experience at school of trying to get into PE and the hockey team, I maybe should have learnt my lesson. The thought of facing that again really scares me. I feel as if I've beaten the bullies and I don't want to risk anything like that happening again. I love taekwondo and nothing would make me give that up, but I used to love PE too. I'd really like to learn more about it. In a previous life, back in my old school, I remember joking about being a PE teacher. It had been one of my favourite subjects and I was okay at it.

Thinking about it has made me feel sad. I feel scared. It has been such a great day and yet it doesn't take much to send me back to those crappy times. I could drop PE now and nobody would know, they'd just think I'd changed my mind. But I would know. There would always be a part of me wondering what I'd missed. I feel a bit better about how I look now so it wouldn't be too embarrassing to do the practical lessons. A few months ago, when the comfort eating was in full flow, there was no way I'd have even considered taking PE. I was turning into a Jaffa Cake and that's not a good look. If it wasn't for taekwondo and Reggie's love of long walks, I'd be turning up for the enrolment day in joggers and a baggy T-shirt.

I've been quite good recently. There was a minor setback on the day before I got my exam results where I did make my way through a whole packet of Jaffa Cakes…two packets of crisps…oh, and enough pasta to sink Italy…but other than that, I've been quite good! What? I was nervous!

I know that the Queen of the Bullies, Nina, isn't going to this Sixth Form, which is a big relief, but I guess some of her gang will be. I bet they're not nearly as brave (or stupid) without her, but I don't want to risk it. Am I going to let them stop me?

I was about to head downstairs to the biscuit cupboard when Reggie came bounding up the stairs. The 'no dog in the bedroom' rule was still working out really well. What Mum didn't know wouldn't hurt her. I was having a little cry and thought he might be coming to sit with me. He's done that before, when I've had bad days, just sat calmly with me as I've cried. Not today. He grabbed the clean washing from the pile on my bed and danced around the room with it.

'Mum's going to kill you,' I shouted as he scattered the clothes everywhere.

He briefly stopped and looked at me as if to say, 'No she won't. You shouldn't have let me up here.'

As I got up to start pleading with him to drop my sock, he raced out of the room and sprinted around the house with it. By the time I finally got him to drop the sock it was a big soggy and I was laughing a lot. I was also knackered.

Reggie had decided that I didn't need to sit and cry. I needed to get off my arse and learn the lesson that PE wouldn't be a bad idea to improve my fitness levels. I felt so much better. Not just happier, but stronger too. If I want to do PE, then I will do PE. If I can get a seven stone puppy dog to (eventually) drop a sock, I can do anything! No more sitting around moping about what might happen. At the moment, life is good. I have Reggie and a soggy sock to remind me of that.

Six

Mum has seriously done my head in today. She's freaking out about me walking to college and even though I wasn't worried to start with, she's now made me wonder if I'll be safe. We ended up having an argument, which was stupid, but I just hate it when she doesn't listen. It started when I made a comment about having to walk Reggie a bit earlier on some mornings. Katie told me that if we didn't have a lesson in the morning we could go in a bit later, so that'll be brilliant for Reggie…and I'll get a lie in. I didn't even get a chance to talk about going into Sixth Form late or getting home early on some days. Mum just talked over me with questions about which way I'd be walking, who I'd be with and whether or not I could take the bus.

I'd spent all morning thinking about which jeans I'd wear for the enrolment day tomorrow. Mum made sure I was no longer thinking about jeans and has me thinking about *that* day. Lightning doesn't strike twice and all that…right? I don't really think about *that* day very much anymore. If there's something on the TV or in a magazine then I try to avoid it, but I've been pretty busy with good stuff. I'm now sitting up in my room wondering if maybe Mum's right and I should be more careful. But on *that* day I was just walking home from school. That's all. Jesus, it's not like I could have done anything differently. It was his choice to do what he did. I hate him for it, and if I could change it I would, in a heartbeat…but what's the point, I can't change it. There was a storyline in one of the soaps a few weeks ago that involved a schoolgirl being raped. It was different as this was by someone she knew, but even though I didn't watch it, loads of people have been talking about it. Mum watched it so that probably hasn't helped her. She has been okay about me walking Reggie and walking to school, but now she's worried. What's that about?

School was only a short walk away and quite often I'd run

home. That wasn't because I was frightened of walking; it was because I couldn't get home quickly enough. Getting away from the bullies and back home to Reggie was the only thing I could think about.

Walking Reggie has never really worried Mum or me. My giant softie who is frightened of rabbits – yeah, I know how stupid that sounds but it's true – definitely looks like he'll protect me from anything. His big Rottweiler face combined with his powerful body and over excitable German Shepherd tail is a force to be reckoned with. Well, it's not as he wouldn't hurt a fly but I definitely feel safe when I'm with him. If it wasn't for Reggie I don't think I'd be out walking on my own so happily. He gave me confidence and made being out in the fresh air fun again. Feeling safe is something I never take for granted any more. I can't take him to Sixth Form with me so I'm going to have to pacify Mum by figuring out which way I'm going to go. This could work in my favour next year as I'll be able to start dropping hints about getting a car.

So Mum has now started going on and on about wanting to keep me safe. It's not like she hasn't done that. No matter how many times we go over *that* day, there was nothing we could have done differently. It doesn't matter how many times I tell her this, or how many times Jane goes over it with her, she can't seem to get her head around it. I always walked home that way; I was just really, really unlucky that he chose that day, that place, that time, to be there too. What am I supposed to do now? I can't second guess every rapist freak that's out there and I can't spend every day being frightened of something that probably won't happen. I can go and try to enjoy Sixth Form. I maybe shouldn't have told Mum that she's spoiling the excitement of leaving school and passing my exams. I know she's only trying to look out for me, but this really isn't helping.

'I'll work out a couple of different routes,' I offered in the end.

'And you can drive me if the times are okay with you getting to work.' She didn't look convinced, and I rolled my eyes. 'And I'll text you when I get there and when I get home.

'Don't roll your eyes at me!' Mum had shouted.

I didn't think she'd noticed. I shouted back, 'I'm growing up and need to be allowed my freedom.'

Reggie lay in his bed, not enjoying the argument at all. It shut me up. He makes me feel bad when he's like that as he looks so sad. He lies really still, with his eyes going from me to Mum. I wonder if we are reminding him of a past he wants to forget, with arguing and raised voices. He was with a mother and daughter who treated him like crap. They were horrible to him and were probably horrible to each other. They didn't deserve such an amazing dog and he definitely deserves better than being in the middle of more shouting. I can't deal with the thought of him being frightened here as he's the only other living being that makes me feel completely safe… I want to do the same for him. I want him to know he's safe with us.

Thankfully, tonight is taekwondo. I need some time out of the house and I always feel better after I've been training. Reggie can enjoy some peace while I'm out!

Seven

I'm knackered. Today was scary. Sixth Form is definitely nothing like school. That has to be a good thing! I sat with Katie and Maya as we had a welcome talk from some of the staff. We had a full on lecture about making sure we'd picked the right subjects. I learned over and whispered, 'What do they think we've been doing all summer? It's all we've thought about. Well, that and what to wear.'

Katie was taking loads of notes and glared at me to be quiet. She hasn't changed.

'I'm still not sure whether or not taking PE was a good idea,' I whispered to Maya, but she just pointed at her notebook where it looked like she was writing a song.

'That was a productive hour,' I added a little bit too loud as they both told me to shut up.

We all perked right up when someone started talking about free periods. Apparently they're not 'free' as they're put in to make sure we have time to study. Yeah, whatever! The first thing we did when we got our timetables was go through our free periods and find out when we could meet up. I've done okay; I have two mornings where I don't have to be in until ten and two afternoons where I can be home early. Reggie will be pleased. We're supposed to be in the library or doing coursework but they said we can go off site.

I'm loving Sixth Form already. If I had the choice of going off site at school last year, I'd never have gone back!

'You know that I'll have to use the free periods to work, don't you?' said Katie as Maya and I were trying to work out if we could make it into town and back on a Thursday. She wasn't joking.

'Yeah, that's cool, we'll have to start the way we mean to go on too,' I replied.

Maya just laughed at us and said she would be doing her music research in town if we needed her.

It's not like I want to fail. I really don't. I want to do well and I think I'm going to like Sixth Form; I just want to have fun too. Sitting there in my jeans, glancing around at all the new people was a good feeling. I was anonymous again. It was better than just being anonymous though as I was sitting there with two friends. Friends! That's something I'm not taking for granted any more. This time last year, I was the new kid in school. Mum and I had moved to have a new start. I'm not saying that was a bad idea, but it really didn't work out the way I'd hoped, the bullies made sure of that. Today, I was just like everyone else. Everyone was nervous and everyone was new. Some people looked like they were there with friends and some looked like they were on their own. I felt for them and did make an effort to smile at a couple of people. I didn't smile too much though; I don't want to risk being singled out again!

There was such a mix of people in that welcome lecture. It's much easier to stand out, or not, when you're allowed to wear your own clothes. As usual, Katie looked like she'd spent all morning getting ready, Maya looked like she'd stepped out of a rock video and I was in my favourite jeans and hoodie. I didn't need to worry about being boring with my clothes choices; there were plenty of other people wearing similar things to me. Maybe we're all boring! I'm all right with that.

I recognised some people who were in my year at school. I felt myself getting quite anxious when I spotted a couple of Nina's groupies, but they didn't even glance in my direction. I was right, without their ringleader they were just the same as me. It was weird; they didn't have that same power over me anymore. I felt a bit sorry for them as they didn't look like they were having as much fun as us three. They weren't really even talking to each other, just sitting there playing on their phones. I felt grateful to have Katie and Maya with me. We did get our phones out to send a selfie to Callie…we were missing her. She replied straight away saying 'Laters, losers…everything you can imagine is real.' I had no idea what she was going on about, but Maya said it was a quote from some famous artist called Picasso! Katie laughed at me for having no idea who Picasso was and then couldn't tell me what he was famous for! Callie wouldn't have been impressed.

We were told to have a look around and make sure we knew where were going in the morning as lessons would start then. If we had any questions, today was our chance to ask them. We went to the café where we spent the rest of the afternoon. I could get used to this! This is the new start I had dreamed of when we moved. It's a year late, but better late than never. I'm almost looking forward to tomorrow.

A new start is a good time to do the goals stuff that I promised Jane I'd do more often:

- It is September and I have my green belt in taekwondo – *not long now and I'll be doing that!*
- It is September and I have started the way I mean to go on with sticking to homework deadlines. *The staff called them assignments today, but it's still homework to me!*

I think two is still enough at the moment! Those two will keep me busy for the rest of the month.

Today has been a big success. I didn't freak out, I wasn't too nervous and I had a really good day. It's the same as what I'm grateful for. Really grateful for a day with my friends, for feeling like I fit in amongst all the other new people and for feeling like this is a real opportunity for a new start.

Eight

Mum's out and not answering her phone. She never goes out and now I need her. I remember her saying something about seeing a friend from work tonight but it is Friday and I don't know what to do. Reggie is limping. He was fine, we had our usual walk and I'm sure he was okay. We got home and I didn't notice anything weird, then when I went downstairs to feed him, he started limping. I've googled it but it could be anything. I remember when I had a bad headache and googled the symptoms; I really scared myself, so I decided to call Mum instead. Why would you have a mobile phone if you're not going to answer it? I know the vet is open tomorrow but I'm worried, what if he's badly hurt? He's lying here next to me, snoring, so hopefully he's not in too much pain. I'm staying with him tonight; I don't care what Mum says.

Okay, try to think about something else.

I was doing really well and started the way I meant to go on with homework (assignments!) but now Reggie has side-tracked me and I'm lying with him in the living room. I suppose I could bring my laptop down but last time I did that he sneezed all over the screen! He's such a classy boy.

I've been doing okay; I've enjoyed having the backup of Maya and Katie in everything except PE. We've been sitting together and Katie is definitely a better influence than Maya. Biology was blowing my brains in the first lesson but Katie was taking notes and seemed to understand every word. That worked in my favour as when we then had to work in pairs, she explained what was going on and I finally got it. Why the teacher couldn't have explained it in simple terms, I don't know. They just have to try to make themselves look smart I guess.

In English, we started on Chaucer and Maya couldn't stop laughing at the fact he's called Geoffrey. It wasn't even that funny but once she started laughing, I couldn't help myself. I have no idea what happened for most of that lesson and am now trying to read a book that I'm pretty sure is NOT English. Seriously, it makes absolutely no sense. If Katie was doing English I'd probably have my own personal translator, but it's Maya, and she just wants to take the piss out of everything. It's fun, but isn't going to help me make sense of the book! She was just as bad in Psychology but at least that was easy to understand and in my own language. I actually really enjoyed Psychology. Jane will be pleased. She seems to think it's harder than rocket science (or Chaucer!) so I won't say that I am finding it pretty easy. Maybe I should give it more than two lessons before I start saying that!

Even PE hasn't been too bad. I was nervous but didn't have much time to think about it. The first lesson was at nine o'clock. Reggie had helpfully chosen that day to run off after a squirrel so I was late getting home. I had to walk as fast as I could to make sure I wasn't late. I made it on time, found a seat and before I knew it, I was there, starting a PE A Level. Glancing around, most people looked pretty fit, but that didn't worry me. The course was a lot of theory but would have some practical stuff too. I was perusing the timetable they'd given us up until Christmas and saw that hockey was going to be part of the programme.

'I hate hockey,' said the voice next to me.

I looked around, not completely convinced the voice was real, to find a welcoming smile.

'Hi, I'm Frankie, I really hate hockey!'

'I'm Dani, and I'm not a huge fan either,' I replied.

That was the start of a fun PE lesson. Frankie hates hockey because she hates team games. 'They do my head in,' she said. 'I can play my heart out, but because some other idiot doesn't give one hundred per cent, we still lose. If I give it everything, I want to win. That's why I started running, it's just me and my legs. If I lose, I only have myself to blame.'

I laughed as I admitted, 'Since I've started taekwondo I'm not bothered about other sports and I'm not really competitive, I just love the training.'

'Woah, taekwondo, you're hard-core. Remind me not to mess with you, although, I could probably run away!'

I didn't bother explaining that I was still quite new to taekwondo. It was nice to have a laugh with someone and it doesn't hurt to let her think I'm hard-core! That could have made all the difference at school last year.

It was such a relief to go back to the second lesson today and have someone to sit with. Frankie is quite like me, she's a mix between Maya and Katie. She's not taking the piss all the time but not taking so many notes that could dictate the entire lesson. I'm glad I stuck with doing PE.

I made it through the first week, laughed a lot, made a new friend and everything has been good. Nobody has a clue who I am, and nobody cares…in a good way! I'm not 'the new kid' like I was last year and for the first time in what feels like forever. I feel like a normal teenager. I hate that word 'normal', but I can't think of a better one.

Now I just need Mum to get home so we can decide what to do for Reggie. He's still asleep, still snoring. I guess that means I don't have an excuse to avoid Chaucer!

Nine

We took Reggie to the vet first thing this morning. By the time Mum made it home last night, I'd fallen asleep on the sofa. I woke up with a blanket over me and Reggie still snoring by my side. I forgot that I was annoyed at Mum for not answering her phone and just sprinted upstairs to tell her about Reggie's limp. He followed me upstairs, proving he was still limping. I didn't think that through.

She called the vet who said they'd fit us in and when we got there, Mum realised she'd put her top on the wrong way around and was wearing odd socks. She's so embarrassing. After a quick trip to the loo, she came back looking a bit better. Reggie seemed fine in himself. He was wagging his tail and trying to say 'hello' to everyone else in the waiting room. There was a cute cat waiting in her basket who hissed at Reggie when he got a bit too close. He certainly understood what that hiss meant and backed right off. The cat's owners laughed at him, saying that despite being small, their cat was usually the boss.

The vet was kind, and thankfully, Reggie behaved. It was a bit of a mission trying to get him to sit on the weighing scales but he got there in the end. After a full examination, she was pretty convinced he'd only sprained his front leg. I felt so bad as he must have done it when we were out together. I didn't notice him doing anything different and promised Mum that I'd been watching him. I really had.

'These things happen, don't worry, he's fine,' she said.

'I bet your mum felt bad whenever you fell over or had a bruise,' the vet added. 'Parents feel bad over the slightest thing, so it's natural to feel that way, but there's really no need. Dogs can have accidents just like we do, even if we're watching!'

Mum went very quiet. She has become a professional at feeling bad because of what happened to me. I get it though. I feel bad and Reggie's only got a small injury.

'Thanks, I just don't like the idea of him being in pain,' I replied, to fill the silence.

The vet gave us a list of things we needed to do to help him get better. Along with drugs and ice packs. She said, 'You can only walk him on the lead for short walks for a couple of days to let him rest.'

'You're joking?' I replied. 'If he doesn't sprint around the park for at least an hour in the morning he'll be bouncing off the walls at home.' I could see Mum mentally preparing for the destruction that would take place in the kitchen.

The vet laughed. 'He'll be fine.'

She gave us some information about other ways we could keep him occupied. She called them 'brain games'… if only Reggie had a brain. He's not the brightest dog in the world. He proved this as we were leaving the vet and he walked into the glass door.

When we got back in the car, I felt a wave of relief. Reggie would be fine. It was the first time we'd had to take him to the vet for an injury and I was so grateful that everything was okay.

Mum must have read my mind as she said, 'God, I was so worried. That bloody dog means the whole world to me.'

Yeah, 'that bloody dog' had completely changed our lives. I couldn't imagine life without him; I didn't want to imagine life without him. I looked at him, sitting in the boot with wide eyes as if to say, 'Well that was fun, it's got to be time for the park now, right?' It was going to be a long weekend.

We got home and started checking out the links to the information on brain games. They actually look like quite a lot fun. It wasn't until Mum then asked me if I was hungry (obviously the answer was 'yes') that I realised it was lunch time and I'd missed taekwondo.

I can't believe now that I didn't even think about it. I'd miss anything for Reggie, but my grading is next week. I've just emailed the instructor to apologise and explain but I need to get loads of practice in. Mum's gone to get fish and chips as she said she can't be bothered to cook. I'm not going to argue with that. I just know that I won't feel like practicing with a belly full of takeaway food. I can make sure I go through it all this evening while Mum is teaching Reggie to use his brain. She said she'd take him for his short walks this weekend as he'd probably be troublesome. I saw her cuddling him when we got home; she looked as if she'd been crying. I sometimes forget that he's not just my dog. I don't mind missing out on the lead walks. I don't want him to think I'm depriving him of park fun.

So far today, I've got a lot to be grateful for and it is only lunchtime.

A reminder that I need to get moving later on though:

- It is September and I have my green belt in taekwondo – *argh, it's next week!*
- It is September and I have started the way I mean to go on with sticking to assignment deadlines. *Okay, so I need to do these over the weekend too!*

I don't feel very successful so far as I've missed taekwondo and am about to eat fish and chips...but I have a lot to be grateful for:

- Reggie only has a sprained leg and will be fine.
- The vet was really good with him...and us.
- I've had a message from Frankie asking about the PE assignment so it looks as if I have a new friend!

Ten

That was tough. Really tough. I have just passed my grading and I have my green belt. YES! Before we got started on the grading, I was able to take my oath. I've wanted to do that for ages and in our club, it's something we do before the green belt grading.

I do solemnly promise to:

- Abide by the rules and regulations of the taekwondo association.
- Strive always to be modest, courteous and respectful to all members, in particular to my seniors.
- Put the art to use only in self-defence or defence of the weak.

Taking the oath made me feel like I was part of the family. I've always felt welcome and I have loved going, but today was different. Taekwondo has been my only sanity in recent months. I was in a bad place when I started going and, other than Reggie, it was the only good thing I had going on in my life. I've worked hard to get to this stage so taking the oath really meant something. I like what it says, I like that it's about respect. If I took that oath into other areas of my life, I'd probably be more successful. It's not that I'm purposely disrespectful, but sometimes I just can't be bothered to make a big effort. I always make the effort with taekwondo though, I wouldn't dare be disrespectful!

Mum was there, watching as I took the oath and as I did my grading. She looked proud as I came out with my new belt, she didn't even make a dig about it being something else for her to pay for. We would have gone out for a celebratory dinner but Reggie's still on his short walk regime so we don't want to leave him for long. Mum even took the morning off work so that he had company while I was at Sixth Form.

I felt completely focused while I doing my grading. I've been nervous about it all day, not really concentrating in lessons but trying to go over all the moves in my head. That was a lot more fun than Chaucer, which makes less sense the more I read it. I told Maya that I was doing my grading; she understood how nerve wracking it would be as she had a similar system for her music grades. 'I just don't get to wear my pyjamas,' she always says. She sent me a good luck message this evening, which was nice.

Frankie sent me a message too, that was a nice surprise. We met up to go through our assignment before class today but it turned in to more of a chat and we didn't get all the work done.

'Is green the one before black,' she asked, almost sounding impressed.

'Uh, no, I've got quite a long way to go before I get to black.'

'That's cool,' she said.

'I've got quite a long way to go before I actually win anything.'

'So, do you know many people here?' She was assuming that I'd been living here for ages. It was a normal assumption as I figured she'd also have loads of friends.

'Not many.'

'Me neither.'

'Wow, so you don't know anybody? It was like listening to my very own cover story a year ago.

'Nope, my folks and I moved here over the summer holiday because my dad got a new job. My older sister's away at uni so my parents decided that it would be a good time to move, not that I got a say in it. I don't really mind as all my friends were going off and doing different things anyway, my best mate's joined the Army but I didn't have the guts to go with her.'

Frankie went on to say she was counting down the days until

she was allowed to visit as they'd been inseparable since they started secondary school. She looked a bit upset when she was talking about her friend so I started telling her about my move. I stuck with the cover story but did admit to hating Year Eleven. The cover story that we moved for Mum's new job almost feels real now. We really moved so that we could both have a brand new start. After the rape, nothing was the same. We could have stayed and rebuilt our lives, but Mum said that she wanted a new start as much as I did. Some people might think we were running away, but I think we were doing what was best for us. It wasn't easy, especially not at school, but I wouldn't change what I have now for anything.

I couldn't believe I was telling her all this stuff as I opened up about the bullies.

'No wonder you're learning to kick some arse,' she said, gently, as I finished by saying I was lucky to know Maya and Katie.

I promised to introduce them all as it was exactly what Katie did for me at school last year and I'd have been lost without them. It was good to be able to do this for someone else.

I sent them all, including Katie and Callie, a picture of me with my green belt on saying, 'I passed!'

Along with nice messages of congratulations, Maya wrote, 'Goodnight, nice PJs.' And Callie sent a message saying, 'Dude, it brings out the colour of your eyes!'

What a difference a year makes.

I need to update my goals, now I need to start working on my next belt!

- It is December and I am ready to take my next grading. *Next time it'll be the green belt with a new stripe.*
- It is December and I am completely up to date with all of my assignment deadlines. *I figured that December was a good*

enough focus for now, it'll mean I'm ready for the Christmas break!

Today has definitely brought a massive success! I'm feeling really proud of myself. I've got a lot to be grateful for too:

- All the support with my grading, from the club, from Mum and from my friends.
- Reggie is doing much better and will be allowed off the lead for a little while tomorrow.
- A new friend!

Eleven

If only I could find a career where I could play with Reggie and do taekwondo all day. A Levels aren't nearly as much fun as I thought they'd be. I thought it'd be really relaxed and I'd have time to do loads of other things too. Nope. Even though I'm only doing four subjects, compared to the long list of subjects at secondary school, they're taking up so much time. If I'm not reading stuff, I'm researching stuff that I need to read, and then I have to write it all down to make notes. Someone has already written it all down and I don't think I'm making a better job of it. It doesn't make any sense.

English is really doing my head in. I used to love reading but they know how to take all the fun out of that. I even had to analyse how many times the letter 'O' appeared in one poem. Who cares? Seriously, who cares? I'm guessing the idiot who wrote it wasn't deliberately finding words with the letter 'O', and if he was, he was in need of some serious professional help.

I am feeling really fed up today. Writing about stuff that I really don't care about isn't helping. I've been ignoring it and doing homework that's a bit more interesting. I'm finding biology really hard but at least it makes sense. Learning about how the body works is cool. We were doing a module on 'movement and support in animals' which meant I could figure out more about what Reggie had done to his leg. It was the first time I'd made a real effort in biology and actually found it quite interesting. I kind of like PE, but only because I have a laugh with Frankie, so that's not a great career plan either. We spent most of yesterday designing a weight-training programme that can develop maximum strength. I have no idea why it took us all day when I could sum up the entire plan with 'heavy weights, low reps, with decent rests in-between'. How did that take us almost a whole day? I don't think we'll be applying to become personal trainers any time soon. We should get the results back in a couple of days so we'll see if that was another day wasted or whether we actually managed to blag a decent grade.

Most of the time I can talk myself into getting things done, but I've been avoiding doing the things I don't want to do. That's just made them even harder as now I have a whole analysis to write by tomorrow and so far I have texted everyone I know, been through my Twitter list and found new people to follow, watched a lot of cute dog videos on YouTube and tidied up my desk…that's how desperate I am to avoid the stupid poem. I have looked at the other A Levels I could take if I dropped English. I can't just drop things when they get hard, I know that, but what about when they are completely pointless?

What's wrong with me? I'm not usually this grumpy for no reason. If I listened properly in Psychology, maybe I'd be able to answer that. I just don't feel as if I'm getting anywhere, that's probably because I don't know what I'm aiming for, but surely I should feel like something is happening, like something is changing?

I work hard for each grading in taekwondo and then I'm bouncing off the walls for like a day. Then it's back to the start as I just want to start working towards the next belt. Before I know it, I feel as if I'm not doing things well enough again and that I should be better. I feel good when I get a decent mark for homework (not that that happens in English), but then it's straight on to the next piece of homework. Nothing is ever good enough. I'm not good enough. I don't know what it will take for me to be enough. I'm just sitting in my little room and the only thing I have to do is write that stupid analysis. If I tried, I could probably write enough to get an okay mark, but I don't want to. I want to spend the evening doing something that matters, you know, like updating my Twitter feed. Seriously though, nobody cares about the stupid poem.

Maybe the poem should be like the first taekwondo belt I got.

It was only Mum who was impressed and before I had even got home, I was planning my next one. If I just get this poem done and ticked off the list, I'll be onto the next thing which might be more interesting. Mum might be impressed, but she's out again so I can't tell her about it. At least I'll have done it. If I don't do it, I'll get a bollocking and I definitely don't want that. I don't think the English teacher will accept, 'But I thought it was pointless, Sir' as a valid reason for not handing in the analysis. Is it about the poem or is it about winning this little battle with my own head? Writing about a poem will never make me feel good enough as I just don't care.

If I win this battle in my head, that will help me to feel better. I said I'd do English A Level so that's what I'm going to do. I don't want to be someone who bails out when things aren't exactly how I want them, so I am going to write the stupid analysis and when I've finished, I'm going to celebrate with some ice cream! Bring it on!

Twelve

I yawned through most of my classes today because I was up so late writing about that poem. Even though I still think it was pointless, I did feel good when I handed it in today. I was so tired I didn't realise how late it was when Mum came in last night. She said she was seeing a friend from work; she's been doing that a lot lately. Am I being really stupid?

Jane called when I got back from walking Reggie earlier on. She was impressed I'd talked myself into writing the analysis. Well done me! She started going on about how I need to be able to make sure I can get on with the things I have to do without spending all day doing the things I really don't have to do. Blah, blah, blah.

'In the real world, you won't be able to sit at your desk messing around on Twitter until you feel like doing your work,' she said.

'I know,' I replied. 'So you didn't tweet me at 11.30 this morning when I guess you were sitting at your desk?' That almost shut her up. 'What's going on with Mum and these new work friends?' I asked. If Jane did know something, she was very good at hiding it.

What if Mum is seeing someone? I can't even think about that. I have been stuck listening to Katie talking about her new boyfriend for most of the day. I can't see the attraction myself. She never just calls him by his name and I don't know what that's all about. She either says, 'My boyfriend, Cal' or 'Cal, my boyfriend.' It's getting really annoying. His name is Cal. Simples. She's really excited and I'm pleased for her, I just don't need to hear every detail of what he has said to her, how many texts he sends and try and figure out the dilemma of whether she should put more than one kiss at the end of her messages to him. Kisses must have some sort of code that I don't understand. She had a total meltdown at lunchtime because she put two kisses at the end of her message to him, and then he replied with only one kiss. She spent the rest of lunch trying to work out what it meant.

'Obviously it means he hates you, will probably dump you and be going out with someone else by tomorrow morning,' was my helpful suggestion. Katie did not find that funny at all. I need to learn about the kiss code as it's a serious business.

I asked Katie if she was going to be around at the weekend and if she wanted to do something. She looked at me as if I was a total idiot and said, 'I'll be with Cal, my boyfriend, he's asked me to go over to his so we can revise together.'

Well, that's not a revision session I want to be a part of so it looks like it's a hot date with Reggie for me. I can't think of anyone I'd rather spend the weekend with!

I did have a good time this afternoon when I should have been researching for my psychology essay. I left early and went to meet Callie before I needed to be home for Reggie. Frankie came with me as she said she would love to be friends with a future tattoo artist. They got on really well so it wasn't awkward and there weren't any weird silences. They both like laughing at the fact I chose a sport where I could wear pyjamas so that broke the ice.

Frankie had grabbed Callie's arm as she shrieked, 'That's an amazing tattoo, did it hurt?'

'Of course it hurt, they all hurt, but it's worth it,' Callie said as she removed her arm from Frankie's grasp. She started walking away before asking, 'Anyone else fancy going to the café?'

'Why don't we all go and get a tattoo?' Frankie suggested. 'It'd be a laugh.'

They both grinned and turned to go.

'I've wanted a tattoo for ages, but I wouldn't know what to have,' I said as I dutifully followed them.

'We'll choose something for you,' said Callie. 'How about a giant koi carp because it's a symbol of strength.'

'Or what about the Chinese symbol for pyjamas because you love wearing them for taekwondo?' added Frankie.

Later I made my escape. I laughed as I left the café saying, 'As much as I'd love to get the Chinese symbol for pyjamas tattooed on my forehead, my dog needs a wee so I'm going home.'

I could hear the shouts of 'wimp' as I started walking home. I texted them both when I got back and neither of them had gone into town, so I'm not the only wimp! They both replied saying how nice it was to meet someone new and that we should all meet up again soon. That would be nice, and having Reggie as the perfect reason to avoid Frankie's spontaneous ideas is even better.

Now that Reggie is back to his usual self we can enjoy our proper walks again. He didn't like his lead walks at all so I was pleased that Mum did most of them. We went to the park this afternoon and got caught in a hailstorm. We tried to take shelter under a tree but that didn't really work as Reggie thought it was a game and started trying to dig up the tree roots. I was watching him, having loads of fun, not caring at all that we were out in torrential rain and hail. He was just happy to be making his own fun and having his own adventure. I was soaked to my underwear, standing under a tree in an empty park and there was nowhere on earth I'd rather have been and nobody else I would rather have been with. As Mum would say, 'I love that bloody dog!'

Thirteen

Should I just ask Mum who this friend at work is? She is spending a lot of time with them and is definitely spending more time on her phone. Last night, we were watching a film and she was constantly checking her phone. She usually makes digs at me when I do that, or if I'm texting while we're supposed to be watching something. I couldn't care less as it meant she wasn't having a go at me for being on my phone; I don't think she even noticed. She hasn't said much about this person and I don't even know if it is the same person she keeps meeting up with. Either she's suddenly become really popular or she is seeing someone, but why would she keep that a secret?

Do I even want to know if Mum has a boyfriend? It even sounds weird for someone of her age to have a 'boy' friend! I'm sure Reggie would have something to say if she brought a guy around here. He's the only man we need in this house.

I've been thinking about Daniel, the sperm donor. I know Mum loved him but he's no more than a sperm donor to me. He disappeared off to find himself and never returned so if he's not bothered, I'm not bothered. Staying in our old house for all those years probably meant that Mum was hoping he'd come back one day, that he'd know where to find us. Well, he has no idea where we are now so I guess Mum has a new sense of freedom. I was never expecting him to walk through the door so it doesn't feel any different to me and I have done just fine without a dad. I definitely don't want that Daniel-Dad and I don't want any dad. I don't need a 'dad' I don't think. What would a 'dad' do anyway? I suppose it's hard to miss something you've never had.

If Mum thinks that she's going to bring some sort of 'dad' in to my life, then she's going to be disappointed. She said yesterday that she wanted to take a couple of days off soon for half term so that we could do something together. That would be cool but I was hoping to spend time with my friends and I suppose I need to finish all my assignments. Frankie was talking about coming over to meet Reggie and coming to the park with us. I'm sure he'd be up for that as long as she can throw a ball and shares her food. He's pretty easy to win over. We're all going into town, too. It's great not being the 'new' friend and Frankie seems chilled. She's going to visit her best friend at some point over half term as she's having her first opportunity to escape from Basic Training. It all sounds a bit scary to me. I can't imagine having to share a room with anyone, definitely not a whole group and I couldn't deal with being shouted at all the time. I don't think her friend is coming here so I won't get to ask her what the Army is really like. I will stick to getting shouted at by Mum to tidy my room or get up in the morning, at least I can just ignore her and nothing bad happens!

I'm supposed to be thinking about what I'd like to do with Mum for a couple of days. Erm, nothing! I don't mind spending time together, but sometimes she wants to 'talk' which is a code for checking I'm really okay, that I'm not being bullied again, having nightmares and that I'm 'coping'.

The only thing I'm not 'coping' with are those talks. I'm fine. I do sometimes have crappy days, but doesn't everyone? I think Jane sets her up with questions and it's like she has some sort of timetable all figured out that explains why I'm grumpy or why I just want to chill out in my room with Reggie and play loud music. Can't I just be grumpy because I have too much homework, because Katie is going on and on about Cal, her boyfriend (!), or because some idiot decided to write a poem that I am unlucky enough to have to read – am I still not over that? Apparently not. So, I'd like to spend time with Mum and have a rule that says we don't need to have the 'chat', we could just do something fun and chill out.

A couple of days away with Reggie would be nice. I'd love to take him to the beach and now that his leg is much better, he'd have a brilliant time. So, if she meant that we could go away, the beach would be top of my list, as long as it doesn't get in the way of my plans with my friends. Mum will probably want to see Jane, which is cool, but hopefully Jane could just join us at the beach and then everyone's happy.

I need to sort out my next grading too. It's not long now until I can go for my next belt and that's something I really want to do. If Mum wants to go away for a couple of days, it needs to be when I don't have taekwondo either! I'd love to practice on the beach, as long as nobody is watching as I'd probably look like a bit of an idiot. Sometimes when I practice, Reggie thinks it's a game and tries to join in; so on the beach it would look a bit weird, like I'm trying to fight my dog! At least if I fell over it wouldn't hurt I suppose?!

I need to stop daydreaming about the beach now and get back on the case with some homework. Wherever Mum is, she can't hear how loud my music is, so that's a good thing!

Fourteen

Oh yes! In record time I have my next belt. I have another certificate to add to the collection and I'm on a mission. I'm seriously behind on my assignments but who needs A Levels when you have a belt with a stripe? I love this feeling. It doesn't last long, but I will enjoy it while it lasts. I worked hard for that belt and even though I think I could have done a couple of moves better, it was good enough to pass. I'll make sure I get them perfect before my next belt. Taking the oath has made me love taekwondo even more, not that I thought that was possible. Being a part of something is an amazing feeling. I even helped with some of the warm ups for the beginners tonight. They were nervous about their grading so I told them a little bit about what to expect and that it wasn't as scary as they thought it would be. Even though that's a bit of a lie and I'm still really nervous when I go for a grading! I hope I helped.

It's now tradition that Mum comes to watch my grading and that we go out for a celebratory dinner afterwards. As usual, we went to my favourite pub and I took on the challenge of finishing three courses. I haven't failed yet! I tweeted a picture of my dinner and had some messages back to say congratulations with Callie being her usual self, saying, 'You'll need a bigger belt, nice one.' Frankie is with her friend at the moment so I'm not expecting to hear from her, although it would be nice. I haven't really heard from any of my old friends but I haven't made much effort either. I get the occasional tweet or 'like' but I haven't made any plans to go and see them or for them to come here.

Mum ditched my beach idea quickly saying that she had lots of jobs to catch up on around the house so thought we could stay here. She did ask if I wanted to go back and see any of my old friends as she has kept in touch with some of hers. That's a big fat 'no' from me. I just don't want to go back to the awkward silences or them trying to keep me involved when we all know that my memories of the place have been changed forever.

'I think it would be too much trouble to take Reggie to the beach,' Mum had said, watching as he lolloped around the room knocking into things. 'There are a few jobs needing doing here at home, anyway.'

'Oh, Mum, he wouldn't be any bother, honestly. I'll look after him.'

'How about going back to visit your old friends, instead?' She smiled as if this was a great idea.

I stared hard at her not believing she could even ask. My mouth dropped open. 'W-what?' I squeaked.

'Of course, we don't have to. I-I mean, I'm not that bothered if – if you really don't want to.'

'The beach would've been fine.'

The thought of going back used to make me feel sick. I dreaded driving past the place I was attacked, or seeing people who had once crossed the road to avoid talking to me. I desperately didn't want to walk past the police station or my old school, both of which are hard to avoid. I don't feel sick at the thought of it all anymore. I just don't want to do it. It's weird but it feels like a lifetime ago, while also feeling like yesterday if I let myself think about it for too long. I feel stronger, more in control, and I wonder if I would feel this way if I hadn't been raped. I wonder if I would just be preoccupied with the little things and not feel as if I'd had to grow up overnight. In lots of ways, that would be a nice.

So, I reckon that Mum was trying out some of Jane's reverse psychology on me as all of a sudden, staying at home to do some jobs didn't sound like a bad idea.

After I've passed a grading, Mum can ask me anything as I feel like I'm on top of the world. I feel strong enough to cope with anything and talk about anything. Tonight was no different and I talked about not wanting to go back but that I didn't feel frightened of the place any more. If Mum really wanted to go, it wouldn't have bothered me, but I wouldn't have joined her and I didn't want her to take Reggie. He's such an important part of who I've become that I don't want the people from my past to meet him and stroke him. I guess that sounds a bit pathetic, but I don't care. Mum said that if she ever decided to go back and visit, she wouldn't take Reggie, even though I don't think she understood why I was making a big deal out of it.

I've been concentrating so hard on my grading and on passing this evening that I'd pretty much forgotten about Mum's disappearing acts. Tonight, everything was normal. Mum said that we needed to 'talk' over the next couple of days but I'm so used to her saying that now, I didn't think anything of it. I wonder what she meant?

Right now, nothing can burst my 'new belt bubble'. I'm lying on my bed with Reggie (Mum will never know he's on the bed with me), ignoring the pile of assignments that I have to finish this week, listening to music and feeling really proud of myself. I'll figure out my new goals another day, but for now, it's all about me ticking off another belt on the road to the one I eventually want, my black belt.

Fifteen

Apparently I'm being childish. If I'm told to keep an afternoon free and there's a comment about 'three of us' having a good time, then obviously I am thinking of THE THREE OF US. Me, Mum and Reggie.

Nope, Mum has decided to tell me that she has been seeing someone – a guy from work called Sammy. This 'friend' is the person that she has been spending all those evenings with and she said that she didn't want to tell me because she 'didn't know if it was going anywhere.'

'So, I'm guessing that now that you've told me, it is officially "going somewhere", whatever the hell that means,' I said. 'I kept tomorrow free like you asked because I thought we were going to head out with Reggie and have a chilled afternoon.' I could feel the anger welling up. 'You can't just bring this Sammy guy along and think that's okay.'

'Dani, he's a really lovely man.'

'Yeah, like you're going to say, "He's a complete tool, but I'm seeing him anyway."' I couldn't keep the sarcasm from my voice. 'Of course you think he's the greatest man that's ever lived.'

'There's no need for that,' Mum said. All I could imagine was this guy who works in the accounts department, dressed like a proper geek, glued to his laptop or reading those newspapers that you need arm extensions to hold open. Yeah, he sounded like a lot of fun.

'I'm nice to your friends when they come over, so all I'm asking is that you do the same and be nice to Sammy.'

She made it sound like some sort of interview, like he's coming over to work out if he can 'cope' with me. I'm not part of some weird package deal, I don't want a dad, I don't want a stepdad and I don't want some bloke in my house thinking he can get involved in my life. Mum can do whatever she wants, but it doesn't have to have anything to do with me.

Mum stayed calm while I was shouting, 'I don't want to spend tomorrow afternoon playing happy families with some bloke I've never met.'

'I understand this is unexpected and you need to take some time to process it.'

'Are you kidding me? Process it? You've been talking to Jane about this haven't you?

'Dani, all I'm asking is that you spend some time with me and my friend.'

'It's not though is it? It's not just time with "you and your friend". Normal *friends* just come over for dinner and then go away again.'

I'd had enough and needed to be on my own.

It's always just been us. I like it just being us. Mum obviously doesn't. She said that she has spent her life looking after me and now it's time for her to live her life. Have I been holding her back from 'living her life' for all these years? While I've been quite happy with it just being the two of us, and even happier now it's the three of us, has she been wishing that she had someone else? Is it my fault that she has never met someone?

I'm scared about what this will mean. Everything will change and I don't want it to change. I don't want to spend the afternoon with Sammy. Mum said that she's been able to talk to him about everything and that she hasn't been lonely since she met him. So has she been lonely all this time too? I know that it's great to have friends, but I didn't think I'd been that horrible to live with that she's been sad and lonely for years. When she said 'everything', I asked her if she'd told him about why we had really moved.

She has. She bloody told him. So, this guy knows more about me than my new friends do. I asked what else he knew and Mum said that she told him how proud she was of me, that I was doing A Levels and that taekwondo had really helped me. Helped me?

Is she SERIOUS? Why couldn't she just say that I loved taekwondo, that I could kick his geeky arse into next week if I wanted to? Why does everything have to be linked to 'helping me'. I don't want to meet some guy who thinks he knows me already, who knows things about me that are really private and now probably just thinks I'm a sad kid who needs 'help'. I don't need help.

I'm not going. I'm not spending tomorrow afternoon with him and Mum can't make me. I'm going to take Reggie out and will make sure I'm not home. He's not going to play happy families with me and he's definitely not playing happy families with my dog. Mum can go and have the time of her life, which I've obviously been stopping her from doing, and I will go and 'live my life' too. I'll take Reggie out for his normal walk in the morning and just won't come back until late. She's going to go mad but she's doing that now anyway, at least if I'm not here I won't have to listen to her. I get the added bonus of having a day out with my favourite boy and hopefully Frankie can come too. I've just sent her a text to ask if she's free and I sent her a picture of Reggie, saying he'd love to meet her. She's replied saying she's coming home tomorrow so should be able to meet us. Sounds like a brilliant plan. No playing at happy families for me, Mum gets to 'live her life' and Reggie will have a brilliant day with me, and hopefully Frankie. That has to be worth getting shouted at for when we get home tomorrow night!

Sixteen

Mum and I still aren't talking. I had the best day out with Reggie and had almost forgotten the text Mum sent yesterday afternoon. I left a note to tell her that I was staying out with Reggie and meeting a friend for a picnic in the park.

Her text said, 'I'm hurt and disappointed that you won't be joining us this afternoon x.'

Ah well, I'm hurt and disappointed that she has told Mr Geek all about me and expects me to just meet him and 'be nice' like it's all perfectly normal.

I was a bit nervous as I left the house. I had a rucksack full of stuff for Reggie: treats, toys, his water bottle, bowl, and a towel because if we walked near the pond in the park, I thought he'd definitely end up swimming. I was right. I took some food and drinks for me too, hoping that Frankie would bring her own as my rucksack was already heavy. I knew that Mum would kick off about my not meeting Sammy, but I just couldn't do it. I reckon she'd have kicked off even more if I'd stayed around and been rude, so actually, this was the best option for all of us.

It was such a good afternoon! Once Frankie joined us, I almost forgot about what I was supposed to be doing. Reggie was amazing and loved Frankie immediately. She had brought some treats with her so she was automatically his new best friend. He also made friends with a little terrier while we were sitting chatting and they kept us entertained for ages. The small cute dog was running under Reggie's belly, which he found confusing. It was amazing that their difference in size didn't matter at all when they were playing. The terrier's mum chatted to us while the dogs were racing around and Frankie said we sounded like proud parents as we talked about our dogs. Yep, I guess I am a proud mum and I don't care how I sound, I love watching Reggie play and then come back to me for some cuddles and a treat. Well, I guess he puts up with the cuddles because he knows he'll get a treat!

I told Frankie about what I was supposed to be doing that afternoon. She laughed and said she'd be totally roasted if she dared not come home for something like that. She also couldn't imagine her mum having a 'boyfriend' if her dad wasn't around, and definitely didn't want to imagine what that would be like! She said that if Mum really liked Sammy, that I'd have to meet him sometime and maybe he would be a nice guy.

'You never know, you might like him,' was her final statement before Reggie came over and shook pond water over us both. He really does have perfect timing. That was the start of a big game of chase where Frankie decided she'd try and outrun Reggie. It never happened and Frankie gave up long before her canine competition.

She did a great job of tiring him out though as he spent the evening snoring and didn't even wake up when he heard the car pull up outside the house.

It must have been Sammy's car as Mum's was already parked outside when we got home, but she wasn't there. I had made some dinner, fed Reggie and we'd stayed in my room all evening. I was a bit nervous about what would happen when Mum got home as I thought she might invite Sammy in and then make me come down and meet him.

I heard the front door shut and didn't hear any voices, then heard Mum make tea and go and put the TV on in her room. She would have seen from the state of the kitchen that we were home. That's something else she can shout at me about when she starts talking to me again.

Mum didn't come and see us and hasn't said anything to me so far today. When I got back from taking Reggie out this morning, I tidied up the kitchen, made breakfast and came back up to my room. I heard Mum go downstairs and talk to Reggie, but she hasn't come upstairs again yet. This is getting awkward.

I'm trying to write an essay but keep getting distracted, wondering if Mum is going to come up and have a go at me about yesterday. Frankie sent a message asking if I was still alive and when I replied saying that Mum was still ignoring me, she said that was even worse! I'm not sure if she's right as I'm enjoying the peace at the moment. I know it won't last forever!

I'm using taekwondo for my essay, but it turns out I prefer doing it than writing about it. I have to explain how rules can help with group dynamics for a psychology essay. I asked Jane for an idea and she asked what the shared rules were in taekwondo. Luckily I asked her before Mum told me about Sammy or otherwise she'd probably have used an example that linked to me having to be nice to him. It was a good tip though as I can write about the five pillars of taekwondo and how they help us all to learn all the skills we need to get better. One of the pillars is self-defence and I've been reading about conflict management as part of how to assess a potential threat. I wish it gave me some tips about how to diffuse the situation with Mum. I am still gutted that she told Sammy the real reason why we moved here and didn't tell me about him sooner so I'm going to happily stay in my room for as long as possible. I just wish I'd remembered to bring some biscuits up here with me!

Seventeen

After a really crap few days, things are less weird with Mum now. I just wish it had been because of something much better than finding out about things going wrong for Amie again. I do feel bad that I haven't kept in touch with her as much as I should have done, but I sometimes just don't know what to say. Even though we've been through the same thing, we're dealing with it in really different ways.

When I first met Amie, soon after she was raped, I was still in a really bad place. I was having the worst time at school, mainly thanks to her bitchy sister, and still figuring out how to get my own head together. Because Amie is a couple of years younger than I am, I think she looked up to me and wanted me to be there for her. I did my best, but I found it hard. It didn't help that her sister was the ringleader of a group of girls who made my life a living hell just when I needed some time to be 'normal'. Instead, I was the new kid in school, being bullied and wanting to curl up in bed and stay there. Amie took those feelings to the extreme when she tried to kill herself and I guess there was a part of me that understood why she had done it. I'm not saying I've never thought about it; but not seriously and definitely not to the point where I thought it would be a real option. What would Reggie do without me? Honestly, in those early days when we first moved here, he was the only thing keeping me going. He helped Amie too, and being his usual amazing self, he was there to help again today.

Mum had a call yesterday evening and things have gone downhill for Amie again. I heard Mum put the phone down, go to the kitchen to make a cuppa and then come upstairs. As we hadn't really spoken properly for ages, I thought she'd been on the phone to Jane and been told that she has to take the first step to be nice. Nope, it wasn't going to be that easy.

Mum handed me a cuppa and said, 'We need to talk. There're bigger things going on than your immature attitude towards Sammy. So for now, we need to put that to one side.'

Wow, what an opener! To be fair, I wasn't sure what to say to that so I just stared into my mug of tea hoping that I'd find some inspiration; I didn't.

'Amie's been fighting at school, self-harming and is now refusing to go to school at all.'

I wasn't expecting that.

Mum continued, 'Her mum thinks that you'd be the best person to talk to her, and I think she wants someone to talk to for herself, too.'

I just nodded, I wasn't really sure what to say and I couldn't let the 'immature' comment go. So I said, 'I'm mature enough to talk to Amie then?'

Yep, even I will admit that wasn't the smartest move. Mum just rolled her eyes as she said, 'I've arranged for us to go over to their house in the morning, after you've been to taekwondo. I think we can put our differences aside for the weekend to help somebody else.'

There's not much I could say to that so I slurped my tea as Mum got up to leave my room.

I felt bad that it had been ages since I'd talked to Amie but I also wondered what I could say that was different to what I'd said before. If she didn't want to listen then, what made them think she'd want to listen now? I know that I was lucky to have Mum and Jane around for me, but Amie has been to see therapists and had support too.

We had laughed as Amie had described one therapist she was taken to see. 'Honestly, Dani, she kept going on and on about self-care but I've got no idea what she meant.'

'What do you want it to mean?' I asked. I had this image of a skinny, aging hippy who thought she was helping when actually she was making everything worse.

'I reckon self-care means eating a lot of ice cream, but that's probably not what the crazy lady meant.'

We had googled her and my mental image was pretty accurate. Her Twitter feed was just loads of pictures about 'being kind to yourself' which made us both want to puke in a bucket. At least it made us laugh.

I had also told Jane about the unhelpful therapist and she said to share the journal idea with Amie; I did that, I even bought her a journal as a present. I told her what I did with planning my goals, writing my successes and writing down what I was grateful for every day – okay, so every day is a lie, I know I need to start doing that again. She promised me that she'd try it but when I asked her about it earlier today, she said that she didn't have any goals, never did anything that would count as a success and definitely didn't have anything to be grateful for.

It was a tough couple of hours. I was buzzing after taekwondo, I had Reggie with me and I thought I could cheer Amie up. It turns out that the only thing that brought a smile to her face was when I asked if she wanted to take Reggie to the park. She said she had no reason to leave the house anymore because the people at school were being really horrible, that she didn't have any friends and her Mum had to call me to get me to come over; I wasn't a real friend either. That hurt. I apologised and said that she was right, that I had been a crap friend. It didn't feel right to say that I'd been having loads of fun at Sixth Form, that I'd met a great new friend and that finally things were going well for me. I didn't want Amie to feel worse about what was going on in her life, but I also wanted her to know that she wouldn't always feel this way if she didn't want to. I couldn't find the words, so we just walked with Reggie. She said that she'd had the best day she'd had in ages thanks to my boy and I promised we'd come back and see her soon.

Her mum had said that there was a date booked in the diary

and that if she tried her best to go to school, then she'd see Reggie (and us) in a month's time. Amie had slammed the door and stomped up the stairs. After saying goodbye, we had left too.

I've felt really bad about it all evening and sent Amie a cute picture of Reggie, saying it was great to see her and we would see her again really soon. I'm going to make more effort and at least text her more often. I hope she goes back to school as she's just wasting her life at the moment.

Uh oh...I can hear Mum coming up the stairs and I bet it's going to be time for another 'chat' as I know she's been on the phone to Jane!

Eighteen

I was right. Mum has just come upstairs for a 'chat'.

My head is still all messed up after seeing Amie and I am now totally overwhelmed by everything. Mum wanted to talk about the Amie stuff to check I was okay and to talk about me meeting Sammy. How was I supposed to kick off about meeting Sammy after the day we've just had? I know that there are bigger things going on and I know that meeting some bloke really shouldn't be a big deal, but it is.

'I wanted to be able to cheer Amie up but I felt totally helpless,' I admitted to Mum. 'I'm angry with myself too because I felt annoyed with her. I don't expect her to be laughing and joking, I know how hard it is when you're feeling like crap, but she won't do anything to help herself.'

'Not everyone's as strong as you,' she said, which wound me up even more.

'I'm not strong,' I snapped back. 'I don't find it easy. I definitely didn't find it easy over the last couple of years…' I thought for a moment. 'Even though life's a lot better now, I still feel like crap a lot of the time.'

I didn't say it out loud but I still freak out when I see a newspaper story about someone who's been raped. I won't watch any TV programmes or films if there's anything in the storyline that would scare me. I have to have Reggie with me when I'm out in the park or the woods or I wouldn't be able to go and sometimes I just don't want to get out of bed.

I wanted to shout that at Amie but I knew it wouldn't help! What are the choices? Staying in bed and feeling worse and worse every day, or getting up, in the hope that something good will happen. With Reggie, there's always something good to look forward to. Without him, I don't know what I'd do. Maybe that's why the only time she smiled was when I suggested going out with him. Maybe she doesn't feel safe otherwise.

What does 'feeling safe' even mean? Sometimes if I'm sitting at home on my own I don't 'feel safe' because I'm thinking about what happened. Then, if I'm walking to Sixth Form and am distracted by the fact I haven't finished an assignment, I am distracted and definitely don't feel 'unsafe'. Amie is always going over and over what happened, she completely defines herself by that one day. It's the reason she 'can't' go to school, the reason she 'can't' leave the house and the reason why she feels like crap. She can leave the house. She did today. If I'd had a choice, I would have happily never have gone to school again but then what? – a miserable life with a crap job because I had no qualifications, no thank you. Maybe Amie is feeling like crap because she wants to feel like crap. That probably sounds stupid but it can be easy to fall further and further down. People like me have the perfect excuse. Something bad happened, so other people almost expect you to be miserable. Seeing Amie today made me realise just how far I'd come, but it wasn't about strength. It was because a life of misery sounds shit. I don't want a life of misery. It's really hard to 'decide' to feel good about what might happen, but it's a lot better than deciding you're going to have a miserable day.

I tried saying this to Mum and she just kept repeating that Amie wasn't able to do that. I disagree. I just haven't figured out how to help her do it. There must be a way that I can help her see that there's another way. Reggie will help, he's the only reason she wants to leave the house so with him, we can go out and talk and have a laugh. With Reggie, she'll feel able to go to the park and maybe even talk to people. It's amazing the amount of people I've chatted to thanks to Reggie, even though I'm usually apologising for him soaking someone, or running off with another dog's tennis ball. That will help her see that there are nice people out in the world too. Christmas isn't far away so we can hopefully plan a time to go out as I'll have more time in the holidays.

Mum finished with, 'It's a good idea for you to take Amie out with Reggie, but I wouldn't push her if she's not ready.'

'Not ready for what?' I asked. 'Who isn't ready for a walk in the park with the most awesome dog on the planet?'

'I'm proud of you,' she answered. 'I'm so proud that you're my daughter and I'd love to take you for lunch tomorrow.' She looked at me hopefully. 'Would you like that?'

As I was nodding she added, 'I'd love for Sammy to meet my incredible daughter, so I hope it's okay that I invite him too?'

That wasn't actually a question as she had walked out of my room before I could answer with a big fat 'no'.

Well played, Mum. Well played.

Nineteen

Today was the day. The day I've been dreading. I met Sammy. I don't think I like him.

I did try to be nice, I really did. Mum took us out for lunch to a new pub which I am sure was Jane's idea. It was neutral ground, not somewhere we'd been before and I had no escape! If he'd come to our house, which I didn't want to happen, I'd have been able to head up to my room but Mum had thought that through.

In fairness, I think Mum was more nervous than I was. She was quiet this morning and being extra nice to me. I woke up to a note saying, 'Enjoy a lie in, I'm taking Reggie on a hike so that he'll be fine on his own while we're out.'

It's not so bad now that I'm in Sixth Form and am home a lot more, obviously using my 'study' lessons properly. I used to hate leaving him alone at weekends when he spent time on his own during the week. Now, he's probably glad of some peace without me talking to him non-stop.

Mum came back and spent a long time getting ready. I put my favourite jeans and hoodie on, which in my world is making a big effort. She tried making conversation in the car but it was obvious that all she really wanted to do was say, 'Danielle, for God's sake please just be nice to him.'

Pulling up at the pub, she said, 'That's his car, he's already here.' She pointed out a really nice sports car. Instead of thinking that the car was cool (which it was), I just thought it was brilliant that he'd never be able to take Reggie anywhere. There's no way he'd fit in that car.

As I got out of our car I got a text. It was Frankie saying, 'Gd luk, b nice & u neva no, u might lk him x.' Yeah, whatever.

I spotted Sammy straight away from Mum's description, 'A tall, handsome, dark-skinned guy who looks like he should be a runner but can't be bothered to run.' That was accurate. I actually felt a bit sorry for him. He hadn't seen us as we walked in and I could see that he was nervous. He was sitting on his own in the corner, with a glass of orange juice, arranging his cutlery. I do that when I'm nervous too. I don't suppose this is his dream of a perfect way to spend a Sunday with his new girlfriend. I thought, *We have that in common at least; neither of us want to be here.*

I liked his hoody, even though I thought he was a bit old to be wearing it. I didn't say that, obviously, but I wondered if he was trying to impress me in some weird way. It looked new. He shook my hand; I must admit that was a relief. I would have freaked out if he had tried to hug me. The only man who has ever hugged me is Grandpa, and I don't really like that.

We sat down and thankfully the waitress appeared within seconds to take our drinks order and explain about the specials. I could have happily listened to her all day so that I didn't have to turn back to the awkwardness at the table.

'Did you get here okay? The roads were quite busy.' Sammy asked Mum. He turned to me. 'People just don't know how to drive as soon as it rains,' he said, then looked straight back at Mum in a mild panic.

Why? Why do people do this? Who cares about the traffic or the weather?

'Have you been out with Reggie this morning? I've heard a lot about him,' Sammy continued, but Mum chipped in before I could answer,

'Oh, well I took him this morning so that Dani could have a lie in, but she takes him most of the time, he adores her as much as she adores him.' She stopped talking, realising that she looked like a bit of an idiot, and started reading the menu.

'I'll take him out when we get home,' I said. 'I don't like leaving him at weekends but he's fine.' Maybe I shouldn't have added the second bit.

We ordered and Sammy did make an effort to talk to me and

ask questions. I was polite; I answered and nodded in the right places. I suppose I should have asked him some things too. I didn't know what to ask and I'm not sure I would have cared about the answers. I was relieved when Mum and Sammy started talking about work as I could just enjoy my lunch and watch the minutes tick past until we could go home.

Mum was happy, which meant my life would be easier over the next couple of days. As we got in the car she said, 'Thanks for making an effort and for talking to him, Dani. I know it wasn't easy for you. I do appreciate it, you know, and you meeting each other is very important to me.'

Annoyingly, I couldn't find anything that bad about him. I'm definitely not in any rush to see him again, but he's not the devil. Mum definitely seems to like him a lot and even though they were keeping me involved in conversations, except about the boring work stuff, I felt like a spare part. I don't want to like him, I don't want him around and I am now very happy to be back at home with the only man I need in my life. My main man, Reggie.

Twenty

If Mum ever finds out what I did today, she's going to go mad. As I walked into Sixth Form, I met up with Katie. She was crying as she'd had an argument with Cal, her boyfriend, over the weekend. Apparently, he wanted to go out with his friends and she thought they were spending time together. I said, 'Oh, I wish I'd known you were free, we could've taken Bailey and Reggie out to the park.'

I don't think that was the response she was looking for. I felt a bit sorry for Cal, her boyfriend, because if she's like this around him that must be annoying. I didn't say that to her as I was relieved she had finally stopped crying.

It was Katie's idea to go into town. I never thought she'd skive off as she's all about getting good grades and working hard. I am too, but never seem to get the grades as easily as Katie does. She does work hard, I'm not saying it's easy for her, just that she has a natural ability when it comes to passing exams and my memory quite often goes completely blank as soon as I turn over the paper. It's why I like Sixth Form as doing assignments and coursework means I get better grades than if it's a memory test in an exam.

'I'll help you catch up,' Katie said, 'but I need to cheer myself up with a day out.'

'You don't have to ask twice,' I replied.

We got on the bus that goes into town.

I was supposed to be meeting Frankie before our first class so sent her a text saying that Katie had talked me into going into town and asked if I could borrow her notes from class later on. She replied, 'No u can't, u cheeky cow. Can I meet u 2 in town? X.'

So, the three of us met up in town for the morning. I did feel guilty for a little while, but then was having too much fun to care.

I thought I could catch up on work later on as I didn't have any classes in the afternoon anyway.

In reality, I'm now sitting at home with the music on, writing this after spending half an hour teaching Reggie to roll over. I need to sort my priorities out. Firstly, finish writing and practice for tonight's taekwondo training!

This morning, I laughed so much I cried. I am not sure if Katie was very impressed that Frankie joined us, but I don't care. She's ditched me for Cal, her boyfriend, over the last few weeks so I'm lucky that I met Frankie and still have lessons with Maya or I'd be friendless again. I haven't seen much of Callie, but we have been messaging and keeping touch. It's weird because I miss her, but at the same time, I am so happy to be out of school, where I saw her all the time, that I'm fine with how things are with us all. I wish Katie was around more, but I guess that's what's happens when you meet someone. If it all ends, no doubt it'll be me she'll come crying to. Can't wait…not!

Frankie is so funny. She decided to join in this morning with some street dancers and she was good, but still managed to wreck their routine. Luckily they saw the funny side and taught her some of the moves while Katie and I sat and watched. They asked us if we wanted to join in too. 'No way, but thanks for asking,' I said.

I had the responsibility of filming it on Frankie's phone while Katie was switching between watching the dancing and staring at her phone in the hope Cal would text; he didn't. I didn't blame him as he'd probably have only got another argument from Katie for not texting sooner. She's hard work at the moment.

Frankie decided she desperately needed a drink after all the dancing so she left her new friends and we spent the next couple of hours in a café. Frankie gave Katie lots of advice on how to deal with Cal, which wasn't very helpful but quite funny for me.

She did make the mistake of saying, 'D'you think you sometimes come across as being a bit "needy"?'

Whoa!

Katie's sharp reply came flying back. 'You don't know me or my boyfriend, Cal.'

Frankie then said the unthinkable. 'We know he's your boyfriend, just saying his name is enough.'

I changed the subject pretty quickly as I thought Katie might cry again.

Frankie has an amazing way of not letting these things bother her and happily joined in with the new subject of me talking about Sammy and how I'd been forced to meet him at the weekend.

It was my turn to face Frankie's blunt advice.

'Just get over it. If your mum's happy, your life'll be easier and that's got to be a good thing,' she said.

She had a point but I still can't 'just get over it'.

Katie joined in by saying, 'I wouldn't mind if my mum found a boyfriend, then she could be as happy as I am with Cal.'

Seriously?! Frankie and I just looked at each other and tried not to laugh while Katie was too busy staring at her phone to notice.

Maybe it shouldn't be such a big deal, but it is. I don't like the idea of a man being around the house. I'm quite happy, right now, with it being the three of us. If Mum's happy, that's great, and Sammy wasn't horrible. She definitely seems happier than Katie, but that's not difficult at the moment. I guess Mum seeing Sammy will also mean she's too busy thinking about him to worry about whether I made it to class today.

Reggie has just looked at me with his cute head tilt, he's right, with or without Sammy, Mum will go mad if she finds out.

Twenty-one

I raced home today, excited that it was the start of the Christmas holiday. I have lots of time to sleep, chill out with Reggie, sleep, practice for my next taekwondo grading, sleep, catch up on assignments, and get more sleep. That was the plan anyway but Mum has already burst that bubble. I'll definitely be spending more time in my room, but that's mainly to stay away from her.

'How would you feel about me inviting Sammy over for Christmas lunch?' Before I could say anything she added, 'Just lunch. We'd still take Reggie out together in the morning and have the evening together.'

Was she joking? She had to be joking. 'Are you joking?' I asked.

Apparently, she wasn't joking.

'I just thought it would be nice,' she said, as if it was the most normal thing in the world. 'Nice for whom?' I replied. It would not be nice for me. It would be close to a Christmas nightmare. Actually, throw in Grandma and Grandpa too and we have everyone's Christmas nightmare.

'Can Grandma and Grandpa come too. It's obviously important that Sammy joins the family?'

The look that Mum gave me was enough to show that it was a definite 'no' to my grandparents being invited for Christmas lunch.

I didn't argue over that as I remember Jane once saying to Mum, 'Be careful what you wish for,' when they were talking about my grandparents not being supportive during the court case. I asked Jane what she meant by that and she said that if my grandparents were being supportive; they'd be doing it in their own unique way which probably meant more criticism. Nobody wanted that. If they were here with Sammy for Christmas lunch, it would be a quick way to make sure he left as soon as possible, which sounded like a great idea to me, but probably not worth the hassle.

It's always been just the two of us at Christmas. Sometimes Jane has joined us, sometimes she's stayed in-between Christmas and New Year, but it has always been us. Mum has always burnt something. We've opened presents while the smoke alarm has been going off and we've spent the day doing nothing, relaxing in our pyjamas and eating whatever we want. How are we supposed to do that with him in the house? I don't want him in the house.

'You're being childish and selfish,' Mum had shouted as I stormed up the stairs, ending the conversation.

On reflection, she's probably right but I don't want him in the house. I can't put it into words that will make sense to Mum. Of course I'm not saying that her beloved Sammy is someone I'm scared of, or that I think he'll do anything. I am scared, that's all. Scared of things changing, scared that there's going to be a man in the house and scared that, well, I'm just scared.

I've been in my room ever since and am getting hungry. I'm not going downstairs though. This is not the way I thought the end of term would be.

I sent Frankie a text saying Mum wanted to invite Sammy over for Christmas lunch and she just replied saying, 'Cool, more presentz x.' She doesn't get it. Why would she? She's got her mum and dad and it's always been that way. I wonder what Christmas would be like if the sperm donor, Daniel, was still around. Would Mum and Daniel still be together? Would we be having a happy family Christmas, or at least a normal family Christmas with some arguments while slagging off my grandparents? I wonder if he even thinks about us, about me.

Daniel Moore…Dan Moore…Danny Moore…there are thousands. I've never looked before and I don't really know why I just did, but how would I even start trying to find him? I don't want to find him. He has never been interested in me so I shouldn't care about him, but I don't want Sammy to be my new 'dad'.

I looked for a while, lists of men with the same name and I had absolutely no idea if one of them was my dad. I was looking at the pictures, wondering if any of them looked a bit like me. How sad is that? I wonder if he has ever done the same thing with my name. If he has, he's never bothered to try and make contact. He could be dead for all I know.

Well, I'm in for a very (un)Happy Christmas. Mum has just marched up the stairs, announcing that she's going out and she'll be back late. It doesn't take a genius to work out whom she's going to see. Before she slammed my bedroom door (now who's being childish) she said, 'You have your own way, Dani, I won't invite Sammy over for lunch. He'll be on his own and I thought it would be nice to offer him lunch, but you can't see past yourself. I don't want him to come here and have a miserable day, which is what will probably happen while you're behaving like this.'

Great. I should feel happy that he's not coming. I'm relieved that he won't be in the house but I don't feel happy and don't feel like I've 'got my own way'. I just can't explain why I'm feeling like this and Mum is now way too angry to listen even if I did want to talk. If she's worried about him being on his own, Mum should go to his house and burn some lunch for him. I'll be perfectly happy here with Reggie and a cupboard full of Christmas chocolate. I know she'd never do that and wouldn't leave me on my own on Christmas Day, no matter how cross she is, but I think I'd actually quite like it.

I bet she's telling Sammy all about what a bitch I'm being. He's probably feeling relieved he doesn't have to come over but I bet he'd never admit to it. Anyway, now I'm home alone I can go and make some dinner (toast)!

Twenty-two

It's been a really crappy Christmas. Sammy didn't come over yesterday and even though Mum was trying to make it an all right day, there were a couple of digs about 'people who are alone at this time of year'. Usually we have a laugh about Mum burning something or the smoke alarm going off. Yesterday, it was just a weird silence while we ate dinner and tried not to say anything that would start another argument. Mum might as well have gone to his house as she spent most of the afternoon on the phone to him, so I went out with Reggie. Even in the freezing cold, I was much more relaxed being out of the house. It was a relief to escape.

Today, we've been occupied so it's been easier. We took Reggie over to see Amie and all five of us (including Amie's mum) went out for a walk. Yesterday was the first time I'd taken Reggie out in a couple of days and I'd missed him. Mum had been walking him, I think it was just an excuse to get away from me, and I hadn't really left my room unless I had to. I needed to do the things I'd been trying to get Amie to do.

I felt like a total loser today though. I've been saying to Amie that she can decide to do the things that make her happy; that she can try and focus by using the diary I'd given her; and that she had choice over how she filled her days. I haven't been doing that over the last few days. I've been in my room, wishing that I didn't have to get out of bed and gradually feeling worse and worse about myself.

I didn't realise how low I was feeling until Amie said, 'Hey, Dani, you're supposed to be cheering me up aren't you? You look like how I feel.'

Who am I to try and advise Amie when I can't motivate myself at the moment?

'It's not that you don't have crappy days, it's that you know how to get yourself out of them,' I said.

'How are you going to do that then?' was her smart arse reply.

'Good question.'

I felt better though just being out of the house. I was trying to show Amie the 'roll over' trick that I'd been teaching Reggie, but he was more interested in trying to find a squirrel that he was convinced had climbed up a nearby tree. I'll never be more interesting than a squirrel, no matter how much Reggie loves me.

We were laughing at him as he had his front legs (or arms, as Amie called them) up the tree and he was half-crying, half-barking at the squirrel who had jumped through the trees and escaped a long time ago.

'So what've you been doing to try and help herself feel a bit better,' I asked her.

'Well, I've written in the diary and it's good as I can say things in it that I really can't say to other people.'

'Can't you talk to the therapist about it?'

Amie pulled a face. 'No way, the crazy lady will just tell me to be kind to myself in her annoying, patronising voice while all I want to do is run out of the session.'

I laughed as I had an image of this woman trying to be 'helpful' while actually just making Amie feel worse about herself. That's definitely not the point of therapy. Writing in the diary had to be a better alternative.

'I do write in the diary too,' I said. 'But, to be honest, I haven't exactly been writing down my goals and stuff.'

'Does it make a difference?' she asked.

I don't have to think about this, it really does. I haven't been doing it for a little while though and I've totally lost focus. I know the stuff with Mum hasn't been helping, but I haven't really been doing anything that well recently. Sixth Form isn't going well, I'm going to taekwondo but I need to do a lot more work for my next grading, I haven't spent as much time with

Reggie as I usually would…and I feel like total crap.

So I answered, 'Yeah, I notice a difference.'

We promised each other that we'd make an effort to do it properly, exactly as Jane had suggested, this evening…

So here goes:

Goals

- It is February and I have passed my grading in taekwondo.
- It is February and I am up to date will all of my assignments for Sixth Form.
- I have not missed any lessons at Sixth Form and been to every taekwondo training session for the whole of January *– no matter what Katie says about going into town!*
- I have spent more time with Reggie, going out for walks, because it's good for both of us.

That should keep me busy in January. This is better than New Year's resolutions as they never work, but I know this has helped me before. I also need to prove to Amie that it works and I know that not writing it down makes me feel like crap, so I haven't got anything to lose.

Success

- I successfully ruined Christmas for Mum. Okay, so that isn't what I should be writing but I don't think I have any successes. That's bad, I need some in January.

Gratitude

- I'm definitely grateful for today. Seeing Amie was more helpful for me than it was for her, I think.
- I am grateful that it didn't rain today so we could have a great walk with my main man. It's never as much fun in the rain. I'm grateful for him making us laugh too.

I feel a bit better just writing those things down, but won't admit to Amie that I couldn't think of a success!

Twenty-three

O.M.G. My head hurts. I've just arrived home from Katie's and need to lie down, with a bucket not too far away. She decided to host a New Year's Eve party as none of us knew what to do to celebrate and her mum was staying at a friend's house. As long as it was only a small group of us, we tidied up after ourselves and she didn't get a phone call from the police, we were allowed to stay over. Bailey, her dog, had a sleepover at our house with Reggie to make sure he was safe, and there was a part of me that wanted to stay at home with them.

Mum sent me a photo of Bailey and Reggie curled up together on the sofa so I think they both enjoyed the evening.

Katie said it was okay to invite Frankie, and Callie brought one of her new arty friends, Hannah. So including Katie and Maya, there were six of us. I'm pretty sure the only reason we were having this girls' night in was because Cal, her boyfriend, had plans with his family, but I'm not complaining as I would have been stuck at home otherwise. I was in charge of bringing pizza, and I am now regretting the fact I also took garlic bread because I can't get the taste out of my mouth. Everyone else brought stuff too but Callie and Hannah decided it wouldn't be a proper party without alcohol.

They made cocktails and had brought vodka jellies. I have no idea if I was even awake at midnight, but I was definitely in the bathroom before the sun came up. Frankie, Callie and Hannah are obviously more hard-core than Katie, Maya and me as we were all sick. It wasn't how I wanted to spend the first day of the New Year.

One good thing about drinking last night was that I totally forgot that Sammy was probably staying at our house. I don't care about him being in the house when I'm not there, but he's not making friends with my dog.

He wasn't here when I came home, but Mum was. She took one look at me and started her lecture about responsible drinking. I would have stayed to listen but had to run to the bathroom. I'm pretty sure I heard her laughing as I ran up the stairs. If this is how you feel after drinking, then I really don't understand what all the fuss is about.

As I found my way out of the bathroom, Mum appeared with a glass of water and some paracetamol. She said we'd talk again later. Great, there's something to look forward to. Katie and her mum are coming over to collect Bailey this evening so we can probably expect a double lecture. We did help Katie tidy up before we left so at least we don't have to prepare for a lecture about that too. Well, I say 'help Katie' but we were all tidying up while she was still being sick in the bathroom. She can clean up in there all by herself!

I did have a laugh last night, but I was having a laugh before the drinks came out. At least I can remember that bit of the night. I remember feeling a little bit out of control, and I didn't like that. I felt safe with the girls and knew that we were okay, but there was no way I would feel safe like that if I was in town. I guess there are some things about what happened that do make me scared when the other girls are just going out for a laugh.

I'm glad to be home, in my own bed. Reggie and Bailey are playing in the garden, which is really cute. I think they'll miss each other. Mum said that they had been inseparable all night and that she hoped we could spend more time with Katie and her mum this year as we all need friends, including Reggie. She's not wrong, and Reggie looks so happy.

I had a 'Happy New Year' text from Amie, which was a nice surprise, and hopefully a sign that she's feeling a bit better. She said that she'd started the New Year by writing in her diary and that I needed to do the same.

Okay, so I've written but need to look at the other stuff too, even though I'm really not in the mood. If Amie can do it, I can definitely do it.

Goals…they're the same but writing them again should kick start my motivation as soon as my headache goes away.

- It is February and I have passed my grading in taekwondo.
- It is February and I am up to date will all of my assignments for Sixth Form.
- I have not missed any lessons at Sixth Form and been to every taekwondo training session for the whole of January.
- I have spent more time with Reggie, going out for walks, because it's good for both of us.

Success

- I successfully cooked pizza and garlic bread. I know that's not much of an achievement but I am quite proud of myself!
- I won our stupid game of musical chairs last night, even though it was mainly because Frankie fell off the chair and I then sat on it.

I definitely need better 'successes' this year as these aren't going to get me anywhere!

Gratitude

- I really am grateful to Katie for last night. Being with a group of friends enjoying a party was brilliant.
- I'm grateful to Amie for her text and motivating me to do this.
- I'm grateful that I am about to start a brand new year and it's full of possibilities.
- I'm very grateful for Mum bringing me paracetamol.

I didn't hear the doorbell but due to the volume of barking, I think Katie and her mum are here. It's time to enjoy the double lecture and say goodbye to Bailey.

Twenty-four

So far so good with the New Year goal setting. I've been training hard and today I was told I'd be able to go for my new belt at my next grading. That's a double grading and I've only been offered the chance because they can see how hard I've been working. I definitely needed to get back to training after eating everything in the house over the holiday. They didn't go easy on us so I think I'm going to be very sore tomorrow.

Now I need to get back on track with assignments too. It's much more fun to work hard at taekwondo! I have a couple of days before Sixth Form starts again so the plan was to catch up, but instead, Jane's here. She was supposed to be here last week but was ill so is spending her last couple of days off with us now. I've escaped for a break as I've already had the start of a lecture on how I'm not being fair to Mum about Sammy.

Jane's totally taking Mum's side on this. I expected her to, but she should be able to understand why I'm finding it hard. Of all people, I shouldn't have to try and explain to her. I just can't find the words. We're all going out for dinner later so Jane can meet Sammy and I've promised to be nice. I don't want to go, but I'd much rather go out than for him to come here.

Jane keeps saying that Mum is really happy and that she deserves happiness with Sammy. I have never questioned that. Of course I don't want her to be miserable, but when someone says that, it makes me feel like I've been the cause of her unhappiness as she gave up her life to raise me. Now that I'm older, she can do what she probably wanted to do all this time. I wish I could be relaxed about it and I will try tonight, but I feel uncomfortable about him being in the house if I'm here too.

I'd tried saying this to Jane and she'd nodded, but then started talking about how change is never easy and that it's been the two of us for so long, blah, blah, blah…

'That's not what I mean,' I had answered, surprised at myself. 'I'm scared about a man being in the house. About me coming out of the bathroom and a man being there. About me being asleep in bed and a man being in the next room.' I burst into tears and ran upstairs. That shut her up, briefly.

'Sorry, Dani,' said Jane. She'd followed me into my room. 'Of course you're scared.'

We'd talked but it didn't make any difference to how I felt about him being in the house, but I compromised with, 'Okay, Jane…I'll make an effort to get to know him. It's becoming more and more obvious that he's not going anywhere, anyway.'

Jane laughed. 'I know your mum really does like him. Your mum likes me too, so her taste can't be that bad.'

I kept quiet as the thought of someone else trying to turn everything into a psychological assessment sounded very tiring. Maybe if I got to know him, it would be less scary to think of him coming over to the house. I wasn't sure it would, but at the moment he could be anyone and Jane had at least agreed that that was a scary thought.

Not freaking out about tonight's dinner was a good start, and it'd keep Mum happy for now.

Jane went on to ask me to list three things I liked about him so far, based on the tiny bit I knew about him.

I did like his car, but that sounded quite shallow if it was the first thing I could think of. I thought about it and said, 'He was nice to me, Jane. He asked me questions about the things I like and wasn't too pushy.' There, that wasn't shallow for a first answer. Then I added, 'He was nice to Mum, too, when we were out.' Oh yes, I was on a roll. Then I couldn't think of another thing so added in that he had a nice car.

I was quite pleased with myself, and Jane went away happy, so it was a win-win. Tonight should be okay as he'll probably be nervous about meeting Jane and about me being there whereas I'm just going to find it funny watching Jane analyse him. The poor guy has no idea what he's in for.

Jane also asked how I was doing with Amie and if she could help. I said there was nothing she could do but that we were both using the diary idea and it was helping. Here goes mine:

Goals

- It is February and I have passed my DOUBLE grading in taekwondo.
- It is February and I am up to date will all of my assignments for Sixth Form.
- I have not missed any lessons at Sixth Form and been to every taekwondo training session for the whole of January.
- I have spent more time with Reggie, going out for walks, and taught him the 'roll over' trick. It's still a work in progress but we're having fun!

Success

- I've been asked to go for my new belt. I'm excited that they can see I've been putting the effort in.
- I came up with three things that weren't terrible about Sammy – that's impressive!

Gratitude

- Even though she can be a little bit annoying, I'm grateful that Jane has come to see us for a couple of days.
- I'm grateful that taekwondo has started again before I actually turn into a Christmas pudding.
- I'm grateful that Jane is coming to dinner tonight so there's less pressure on me.

Okay, it's time to find my favourite jeans and a different hoodie, after all, I'm the only one young enough to be wearing one!

Twenty-five

Back to real life now.

I said 'goodbye' to Jane this morning, went back to Sixth Form and now have a long list of assignments I need to finish. The holidays are definitely over.

I had the worst time out with Reggie tonight too. It was dark when I took him for his walk so it wasn't the most fun for either of us, then I picked up his number two and found there was a hole in the bag. So disgusting. I swear that I'm getting through all the crap stuff at the start of the year – literally! I still don't feel great and all these little things keep happening to mess up my day.

Anyway, back to this morning. Walking into the first lesson of the New Year, I was asked for my assignment. 'What assignment?' It turns out I'd written down the wrong date in my diary and it was due in today, not at the start of February.

My head just isn't switched on. I'm going to lose marks because it's late and I have to get it done and handed in by next week. How am I supposed to do that? I need another holiday, but this time, I actually need to do some work.

I spent the last couple of days with Jane as well and didn't get much done at all. Sometimes I'm not sure if talking about things brings it all back rather than focusing on the future and some good stuff.

We, Jane and I, were talking about Sammy and about Amie, which led us back to how I'm feeling and about things that I probably wouldn't be worried about if it wasn't for what happened. I wouldn't be talking with Amie if I hadn't been in a similar situation to her and I'm not sure I'd be so worried about Sammy being in the house. I'm pretty sure that I would still feel uncomfortable about it all and not want a new 'dad', but I don't know if I'd be scared.

To be fair, nobody has said anything about him being a new 'dad'. Jane was surprised I'd even thought about that. I hope she hasn't said that to Mum as that would be embarrassing. I just can't help thinking about these things.

Jane said that I was doing a great job with Amie and that I needed to realise it wasn't my responsibility to help her. I could only say what I felt was right and then it was up to Amie whether she tried the things I'd mentioned.

I know that Jane's right, but I just wish I could get Amie to see that life could be so much better than it is now. When I was talking to Jane, I realised that I needed to remind myself of that too. I do feel quite down a lot of the time and I know that the arguments with Mum aren't helping. I used to love being at home, but now I'm spending more and more time in my room. I don't want Mum to think she can't talk about Sammy, but I am worried that she's going to say he's on his way over to our house. I'm sure she'd tell me and he wouldn't just appear one day.

That evening with Sammy was okay actually, he was definitely nervous about meeting Jane which was quite funny. She didn't ask any weird 'psychologist' questions but he seemed to think she was analysing him anyway. He thought about everything before he answered her and looked at Mum a lot as if to ask if it was the 'right' answer. She only asked where he'd gone to university! Jane did most of the talking so I could stay quiet, enjoy my dinner and not say anything that could get me into trouble. Nobody mentioned Christmas Day so that was good as that could have been awkward. I know that Mum will have told him why he wasn't invited, but he was nice enough not to say anything, which was cool.

He had asked if I'd enjoyed the New Year's Eve party. Mum had obviously told him about my headache and visits to the bathroom. He'd thought it was funny and had said, 'It's a few nights like you experienced that's led to me only drinking this…' He pointed to his orange juice.

'I don't blame you,' I had answered, and meant it.

The evening wasn't as awkward as the first time we met, mainly thanks to Jane's ability to talk non-stop.

Back in the car, she then dissected her thoughts on Sammy with the conclusion being, 'Yeah, I like him, I think he's good for you.'

Phew. I wonder what Mum would do if Jane had said she hated him and thought they should split up straight away? Wishful thinking.

I need to get on with my assignment. I now have even more work to do and I'll be gutted if I have to miss taekwondo this week. My only goal at the moment is finishing that assignment, and all the others that I should have done over Christmas.

I keep telling Amie that it's even more important to write when you don't feel like it, so I'll do what I have asked her to do.

Goals

- It is February and I have passed my DOUBLE grading in taekwondo.
- It is February and I am up to date will all of my assignments for Sixth Form.
- I have not missed any lessons at Sixth Form and been to every taekwondo training session for the whole of January.
- I have spent more time with Reggie, going out for walks, and taught him the 'roll over' trick properly.

It's going to be a mission to achieve these.

Success

- I was nice to Sammy when we went out for dinner.
- I didn't cry when I realised I hadn't done the assignment.
- I didn't cry when I realised there was a hole in the poo bag!
- I have written this.

Gratitude

- I'm grateful for the time with Jane.

Twenty-six

Feeling like a hypocrite today! We'd arranged to see Amie and her mum this afternoon so I decided I'd spend the morning working on the assignment. It's amazing how quickly the time disappears and how I find so many more interesting things to do.

I had a lie in, Reggie had a longer walk than usual and I even tidied up the massive pile of clothes on my bedroom floor that Mum had been nagging me about for ages. I found time to go through some practice for my grading and found time to watch half an hour of a (not very) interesting cooking programme on the TV while I had breakfast. I couldn't find the time to do any coursework though – weird!

So, who am I to be talking with Amie about working hard, trying her best and taking small steps to work towards what she wants in life? I definitely didn't do any of that this morning, except for taekwondo, but I can always find time for that.

Amie is finding it tough, but I have to give her credit because she really is trying. She has only missed one day of keeping her diary since we last saw each other, she has been back to school and has plucked up the courage to talk to her mum about getting a new therapist. That was quite funny as her mum's reply was, 'Definitely, darling. I'll look into it today. I thought she was a bit nuts too, but didn't want to upset you if she was helping!'

Her mum has sorted out a couple of new people for Amie to meet to see how she feels about them. How cool is that? If only we could all have the guts to be honest from the start.

Amie didn't want to give her mum another reason to think she wasn't trying and her mum didn't want to upset Amie. All along, they were thinking the same thing!

I was lucky as I had my own personal head-fixer in Jane (she'd kill me if she knew I'd written that!), and still do have her; but when you're talking about something so personal, you have to be able to trust the person in front of you. It's not just about trusting them to keep things private, that's almost a sure thing in their work, but you have to be comfortable with them. You're sharing your biggest fears, your hopes for the future, the most painful experience of your life, your heart and soul. If you're sitting in front of some muppet who can't get past the wise words of 'look after you', then they don't deserve your trust. Having the guts to say to her mum that Amie needed something different and still really wanted to try to get through this with help, is amazing.

This afternoon, as we were out in the freezing cold park with Reggie, Amie admitted, 'I'm actually excited to meet the new people and see which one I get on with.' She smiled. 'I feel like I have the choice now.'

I never thought I'd hear her say she was excited about it! I'm really pleased for her.

When I'm out with Reggie, I often get the best thoughts pop into my head. Today, I remembered something that Jane had said while she was staying with us and I shared it with Amie. '… it's a bit like taekwondo, it really hurts sometimes when you're training but you know it's worth it because you're getting stronger and getting better at the sport you love.' I paused to let that take effect, then continued, 'So, even on the days when the memories hurt or when you're frightened, working through it and figuring out a way forward makes you stronger and gives you quicker solutions if it happens again… You're training yourself for the life you want, and living the life you want.'

Amie thinks I'm seriously smart, but I'm usually only repeating what Jane has told me, so I added, 'It's what Jane said, actually.'

Her reply was funny. 'Jane's probably just repeating something she read, or that someone said to her!'

She had a point! We could all be talking complete and utter rubbish, but who cares, if it helps? It has helped me and I hope it's helping Amie. The thing for me is remembering that I need to do these things every day. Like with taekwondo, I don't practice once and then never have to practice again. If I don't practice for a couple of days, I can feel myself missing things or having slower reactions when I try again. Why would it be any different with keeping the diary or doing things that help me to feel better? Why the hell can't I remember this when I'm sitting watching the stupid cooking programme?

'To be honest, Amie, I've wasted the whole morning and totally messed up the deadline,' I had admitted.

'At least you made it to class last year,' she'd answered. 'This year, you have to practice listening and actually do the work too!'

That's true! So, once I've finished this, I'm going to focus on that bloody assignment.

Goals

- It is February and I have passed my DOUBLE grading in taekwondo. *I'm practicing every day; I really want this!*
- It is February and I am up to date will all of my assignments for Sixth Form. *Starting with the one I should have finished last year!*
- I have not missed any lessons at Sixth Form and been to every taekwondo training session for the whole of January.
- I have spent more time with Reggie, going out for walks, and taught him the 'roll over' trick properly. *I've done the first two so far, need to do the third!*

Success

- I helped Amie (I hope)

Gratitude

- I'm grateful for the time with Reggie and Amie.
- I'm grateful for Amie helping me too. She made me laugh and didn't make me feel like a hypocrite!

Right, no more excuses…!

Twenty-seven

I have made a decision! There, that's my success for the day!

Seriously, I am pleased with myself. I'm still thinking about Sperm Donor Daniel a lot and have done some searches for him online. I don't know why as I've never wanted to look for him before, but since the whole Sammy thing started, I've wondered what it would be like to have my own dad. I know that I don't want a 'new' dad but I don't even have an 'old' dad. Maybe it was naïve to think it would always just be the two of us, but I hadn't thought about a guy being part of our lives at all.

I haven't found him, but I have found ways that I could get help to find him or ways to look into my family tree. According to one of the websites, finding out about my ancestors will gave me a better understanding of who I am. Is that true? I know who I am. I do things that I know definitely come from Mum, but she's been with me every day of my life. Some bloke who ran off when I was a baby can't have had that much of an impact. And even if I've got some bits of his genetically, that won't change whether I know him or not. One thing I am sure of is that finding him would take a lot of time and effort. I already don't seem to be able to find the time to do my coursework and build a future so I'm not sure there's any point in wasting time finding out about my past.

I don't know if he'd even want me to find him. He has never tried to make contact so it would be pretty horrible to find him and for him to then say that he didn't want anything to do with me. At least this way, he's already made his decision and I haven't lost anything. You can't lose what you have never had, and until recently, I haven't been bothered. I'm not sure I'm that bothered now, it's just been bugging me a bit. I might just be finding another way to avoid coursework as I'm good at that.

What if I did find him, he wanted to meet and we started

talking to each other? What would be the point? I would want to know why he left and why he broke Mum's heart. I'd want to know why he never got in touch and whether he's even thought about us in the last 16 years.

I remember asking Jane a while ago, to find out if she had any idea why he did it. Her reply was, 'Because he's a selfish prick.' She immediately apologised and said she shouldn't say that about my father, but that she could never forgive him for how much he hurt my mum.

I talked to Frankie and Katie about it and they both agree that he doesn't deserve for me to go looking for him.

'In fairness, you lived in the same house for like, fifteen years. If he wanted to say "hi" it wouldn't have been that hard,' was Katie's first response.

'Screw him,' were the words of wisdom from Frankie.

What would I do without them? Talking to them did help. They both have different experiences to me. Frankie's mum and dad are still happily married and she's always had them both around. Katie knows her dad but doesn't have much to do with him and it's just her and her mum (and Bailey) in the house.

Frankie added to her wise words by saying, 'I guess it would be different if you didn't know anything about him at all, and then it might be interesting to find out if he's a rock star or a famous footballer or a millionaire. But you already know he's a waste of space, so there's not much point.'

I know that he broke Mum's heart and I haven't said anything to her about what I've done or that I've been thinking about him. She has never kept anything a secret so I know a bit about him. I know his full name. I know he likes sport and green tea (weirdo), and she did tell me his birthday but I've forgotten it. I also know that he ran away from the woman he said he loved and his daughter without ever coming back to see if they were okay. Is that really a man I want to go and find? I think Frankie and Katie are right in what they said.

Things haven't been great with Mum and I don't want her to think that I'm trying to annoy her or get back at her. He has just been on my mind a lot. I can't imagine how hard it must have been to be dumped and left to raise a kid on your own. It must have been scary and she had to get over him while making sure I was okay too. Katie can't even cope for thirty minutes without checking to see if she's had a message from Cal, her boyfriend, so imagine if he just disappeared. I don't think I could cope, never mind Katie!

My decision is that I am not going to look for Daniel and I feel good about that.

Goals

- It is February and I have passed my DOUBLE grading in taekwondo.
- It is February and I am up to date will all of my assignments for Sixth Form. *Argh, this one is so boring!*
- I have not missed any lessons at Sixth Form and been to every taekwondo training session for the whole of January. *I'm doing well with this one. 100 per cent so far!*
- I have spent more time with Reggie, going out for walks, and taught him the 'roll over' trick properly.

Success

- I made a decision! I think that was partly down to talking to Amie and hearing how happy she was about taking control of her own decisions. I am not looking for Daniel.

Gratitude

- I'm grateful for having Katie and Frankie to talk with.

Twenty-eight

So, Reggie is rolling over like a professional. I have no idea how many professionals need to do this but he is a genius. He is so cute and looks very pleased with himself when he's done it, sits back up and gets a treat. I only ask him to do a couple of rolls every day, now that he's learnt it. I was getting really excited and asking him to do a few at a time until Mum said I'd be making him dizzy.

Mum saying, 'If he's sick, you're going to clean it up,' was enough to make us stop for the day. That's one goal ticked off the list. It's not surprising I ticked this off the list first as it was the one that was the most fun.

Reggie's not the only successful family member either. I HAVE MY BELT! I'm now closer to my black belt than ever and it's definitely getting harder. Getting my green belt and taking my oath was a massive step forward for me, but being chosen to go for a double grading was extra special. The fact that they could see I've been working hard really matters to me as it makes it all worthwhile. I know that I started taekwondo for myself and to help me feel better about everything, but when someone else can see that you're trying hard and gives you a chance to get even better, that's very cool. I think the coaches are amazing, so when it's someone you respect who gives you that chance, it is extra special.

I did have an argument with Mum last night, which meant I wasn't as focused as usual before the grading. It's become of a bit of a routine that Mum goes out for dinner with Sammy on a Thursday, which is the same night that the grading was booked for.

Last night, she asked, 'What time do I have to be there to watch you?'

'Don't bother, you don't have to be anywhere,' I'd snapped

back. 'It's your night with Sammy and I don't want to get in the way of that.'

I hadn't meant it to come out quite like that; I just didn't want her to bring him along because that was the time they spent together and if that was the option, I'd rather she didn't come at all. It turned out that most of that was only happening in my own head.

She wasn't impressed with what I said and shouted, 'You really do need to grow up and realise that not everything revolves around you. I've always supported you and tomorrow night won't be any different.' She'd slammed the kitchen door and marched upstairs.

She left her cup of tea and I knew she wouldn't come back and get it because that would spoil her dramatic exit. She didn't, so I congratulated myself on being right about it and drank it for her. I wasn't sure if that meant she was definitely coming or not, but she wasn't home at the usual time today and I figured she had decided to go out with Sammy.

I did manage to concentrate in class today. It's hard not to when there's so much to learn if I'm going to pass these A Levels.

'I've got my grading tonight', I told Frankie.

'Are you at black yet? I'll be impressed when you get to black.'

I hoped she was joking as it's going to take me a long time to impress her.

'Good luck though, I hope you nail it,' she'd said, before I came home to get ready.

I took Reggie out and we had our tradition pre-grading pep talk. Which is where I take him for a long walk and talk the whole way around about what I need to do, what I'm worried about, which bits I find the hardest and how I really want to pass. He listens, runs after things, makes me laugh and I always come home feeling better about it all. This afternoon was no exception. Reggie 'helped' while I went through everything for the final time in the living room. He 'helps' by getting under my feet, bowing at me because he wants to play and jumping around like he's joining in. It's a great way for me to practice getting it right while there's a big distraction in the room. There still wasn't any sign of Mum so I made something to eat and got ready. I walked to the session myself and couldn't see her car so just went in and got changed, pretending that I didn't care. Everyone is nervous at these sessions so I was occupied and enjoying watching the others going through their grading while I waited for my turn.

I was called in and had one last look in the spectator's area. Mum was there. I was relieved as she smiled and mouthed the words 'good luck' as I got started. The nerves disappeared as I found my rhythm and all the preparation paid off. It feels amazing to have my new belt, a double grading and be a massive step closer to the ultimate goal. Mum didn't say anything about last night's argument and stopped for our favourite takeaway on the way home as a treat. It's been a pretty awesome day.

Goals

- It is February and I have passed my DOUBLE grading in taekwondo. *YES I HAVE! Now to start working towards my next one.*
- It is February and I am up to date will all of my assignments for Sixth Form. *Done…almost… Okay, so I'm still behind on one, but that's not bad!*
- I have not missed any lessons at Sixth Form and been to every taekwondo training session for the whole of January. *Done!*
- I have spent more time with Reggie, going out for walks, and taught him the 'roll over' trick properly. *Done!*

Success

- Reggie knows how to roll over when I ask him to!
- I passed my double grading and have my new belt.

- I had a nice evening with Mum and we didn't argue.

Gratitude

- I'm grateful for living with the most amazing dog on the planet.
- I'm grateful to Mum for coming to watch and for our takeaway.
- I'm grateful that she didn't bring Sammy!

Twenty-nine

Today has been a challenge. I have been forced to listen to Katie go on and on and on about Valentine's Day. She seriously hasn't talked about anything else. 'What should I get him?', 'What should I wear?', 'What do you think he'll get me?', 'What if I get him something romantic and he gets me something he thinks is funny?' ... 'What if, what if, what if...'

'I DON'T CARE!'

She still can't manage to say Cal's name without adding 'my boyfriend' and even when I put my iPod on and turned the volume up, it hadn't stopped her talking. I'm not sure she would have noticed if I had just got up and walked away. I wish I had tried that. I don't want to be annoyed with her but I just don't get what all the drama is about. It's just another evening with the same guy she's been seeing for what feels like a lifetime.

I can't say anything because I'm supposed to be a friend and supposed to be happy for her, but she's too much when she's like this. I sent Frankie a message at lunch time asking her to come and save me from Katie's constant boyfriend chatter and she just replied saying, 'Not on ur life, I can't cope wiv her on a gd day so wen shes like dis I might end up behind barz x.'

Katie hadn't even noticed me laughing at my phone; she would usually get all paranoid and want to know what I was laughing at.

If I'd said that she was getting annoying and maybe taking it all a bit too seriously, she would probably have only thought I was jealous. Maybe I am? I don't think I am though. I can't imagine wanting to be like Katie over some boy. Cal's a nice guy and I have a laugh with him, but I don't get what the big deal is.

Maybe if I hadn't had all that crap happen, I'd feel differently about it. Maybe there's something in me that's now scared. I'm definitely worried about Sammy being in the house, but I'm not scared of the guys in Sixth Form or the guys at taekwondo. I really like having a laugh with them but I've never looked at them 'like that'. I've never thought I'd like to go out with them and when Katie is going on and on about how gorgeous Cal, her boyfriend, is, I just don't see it.

She wouldn't stop talking about how much she liked kissing him the other day and laughed at me when I said, 'Isn't that a bit itchy because he's got that stubble all over his face?' I thought it was a fair comment but she just thought I was being funny. I'll take it that either it's not itchy or she doesn't care that it's itchy. Either way, I don't really understand what all the fuss is about.

I have never thought about kissing any of the boys that I like having a laugh with. Even Amie has talked about a guy at school she thought was really nice. I didn't think about it at the time as we were laughing about whether she'd have the guts to ask him out and she went red as she shouted, 'No way.' As she'd shouted, Reggie wondered what was happening and ran back to us at superfast speed and almost knocked Amie over so that made us forget all about her possible new boyfriend and gave us something different to laugh about.

I wonder if things had been different if I'd be more interested in getting a boyfriend. When all my friends were starting to get really interested in boys, I was in the middle of trying to get through the court case and much more worried about how they were talking about me. And although they tried to be nice, it was so awkward all the time. I don't remember them talking about boys much but maybe they kept quiet because they didn't want to upset me. Maybe I just wasn't listening because I was trying so hard to be 'normal'. Then, when we moved here and I moved schools, I didn't have anything to do other than get through each day and try and avoid the bullying bitches. I didn't care about anything other than passing my exams and never going back to that place ever again. It's not really surprising that boys haven't been an important part of life so far.

I guess it would be nice to have someone to go out with on Valentine's Day. When I see myself with someone, I just don't know who it is. There's a blur and it definitely isn't a blur that looks like any of the guys I know. It's a bit sad that I'm sitting here with Reggie and even Mum has a date on Valentine's Day. Maybe I should care more than I do but I'm happy here with my boy!

Jane called earlier to say 'hi' and said, 'I'm at home with a takeaway pizza and a bottle of wine, at least you have Reggie.' Yep, she has a point!

Goals

- It is April and I have my red belt in taekwondo.
- It is the end of half term and I am up to date will all of my assignments.
- I have taught Reggie a new trick, need to figure out which one.

Success

- Not shouting at Katie. I actually think I deserve some sort of medal for that.
- Getting a date with the most handsome boy on the planet on Valentine's Day! Who cares that he's a dog!

Gratitude

- I'm grateful that I'm here with Reggie and feeling really happy about that, as sad as that might sound.
- I'm grateful that Mum's going to be late home so she won't be able to ask me about my assignments, which I haven't done.

Thirty

I haven't left the house since I came home from Sixth Form two days ago. Mum thinks I'm ill, which is fine by me. She said, 'I always know when you're feeling really poorly as there's no other reason you'd miss taekwondo.'

Yeah, all right then.

There is another reason. I can't sleep, I feel sick and I have felt that way ever since it happened two days ago. Well, I say 'it happened'. Nothing happened, but I still had a total meltdown and freaked out before running all the way home crying more than I've cried in months. It was so stupid. Nothing happened.

I was walking home along the road that runs along the park. It was the afternoon and nothing was weird about it at all. The bus stopped on the other side of the road and as I walked by, I noticed a guy get off the bus and look at me. I actually have no idea if he looked at me or if he was just looking in my direction, but I still noticed him. He was wearing a hat that was covering the top of his eyes and a long dark jacket. His rucksack looked older than me and he definitely needed to shave. There was just something about him that made me look twice.

As I looked back, he was crossing the road and heading in my direction. I'm sure he looked at me again. I reached for my phone and it wasn't in my pocket which made my heart race even faster. I had promised Mum and Jane that when I was walking on my own I would never listen to my iPod, I wouldn't text or message on my phone, I would stick to main roads and I would make sure I had quick access to my phone so I could call someone if I was worried or needed help. I always had my phone in my pocket so where was it?

I sped up and could hear him walking quickly behind me. Nobody else was around and I had nowhere to go but keep walking. I could feel every inch of me starting to panic and where the hell was my phone? I needed to call someone. I needed to be ready to phone 999. I NEEDED MY PHONE.

The last thing I did at Sixth Form was show Frankie a picture of Reggie trying to climb a tree after a squirrel. I don't think she cared but she was nice enough to look at the picture and say he was cute: stupid, but cute. I only heard 'cute'. I must have just thrown my phone in my bag with my books and pens. It had to be in my bag.

As I dropped my rucksack off my shoulder to reach inside for my phone, the man walked past me. He was too close to me and I could smell him as he must have been just millimetres away. I froze.

He didn't even look in my direction. He was staring down at the ground and marching straight ahead. I am not sure he even noticed me. I couldn't move.

Then I cried.

What the hell was that about? After what felt like forever, I could see that he was in his own little world, walking so fast that he was already turning on to the main road that leads to the other side of the park. He was no threat to me at all and never had been. I found my phone but had no idea who to call. What would I say? 'A man just walked past me on the street.' I'm not sure that anyone would care. I felt stupid but clung on to my phone as I made my way home.

I don't remember the rest of the journey home but I was still crying as I climbed the stairs and got into bed. Mum came home and asked what was wrong, but quickly left me alone when she realised she didn't have long to take Reggie for his walk before it got really dark. She brought me some toast and a drink of water but I wasn't hungry and she said she'd stay in so if I needed anything, she'd be there. I pretended to be asleep whenever she came to check on me. It was a great way of being left alone, but it also meant she wouldn't let Reggie in. I could hear her talking to him. 'Ahh, gorgeous boy, she needs her rest so you'll have to settle for cuddles with me instead.' I really wanted Reggie cuddles!

As Mum left for work this morning, she said that if I was still poorly when she got home she was going to call the doctor. I've sent her a text saying I feel a bit better, which is sort of true, but I'm scared it will happen again. I totally freaked out and there was no reason for it. I must have seen loads of men getting off buses as I've walked around and must have had men walk past me before too.

Frankie has been texting and Katie and Maya have said they'll come over but I've replied saying I've got a tummy bug and don't want them to catch it. That's always a good excuse and makes sure nobody wants to come near you. They'll let me read their notes because I've missed some classes but I'm going to go in tomorrow. Mum can drop me off on her way to work and I'm going straight to taekwondo for an extra training session in the afternoon. I'm not sure if Mum knows about that as I usually go in the evening. Who cares, I've been looking forward to it and it's the only thing that'll make me feel better.

I really hope I can sleep better tonight. I keep waking up and then can't get back to sleep. At least I'm not feeling sick any more so Mum will hopefully be happy to cook a nice dinner as I can't eat any more toast. I am not going to tell her about this as we're still not getting on like we used to. She'll just be pleased that I'm feeling better. Reggie won't be happy that he's not spending the days curled up with me, but I am fed up with feeling this crappy and need to sort myself out.

Thirty-one

Seriously, this week can't get any worse.

It took everything I had to get up and go to classes this morning. 'You look like death,' was the caring way Frankie welcomed me back. When I just looked at her and didn't say anything she added, 'Sorry, babes, you still look pretty rough, I mean poorly, are you okay?'

'I'm not contagious, don't worry,' I said as I slouched into my seat and tried to find my book. At least I had remembered the right book so all I had to do was open it on the right page and pretend to be reading. I did well.

I had no idea what the lesson was about but I knew which pages I had to read before next week. That was easy enough. Frankie was nice to just be quiet and not keep telling me how horrible I looked. I was surprised by how gutted I felt when she said I looked 'rough'. It was nice to have company without having to make any effort to talk or pretend everything was okay.

I had some time to kill before I could go to the early taekwondo session. 'I'm just going to go to the library and get some work done,' I said to her.

'You really must be ill,' she replied as she headed in the direction of the drinks machine. 'Catch ya laters.'

It was quite nice in the library. I've never spent much time there before but it's where people go to listen to their iPods and doodle pictures while they're surrounded by books they can't be bothered to read. Nobody tried to talk to me, nobody cared that I was sitting on my own in the corner, and nobody told me I look 'rough'. I might go there more often. There was a part of me that didn't want to leave. I felt safe there and even though I wanted to go to taekwondo, I didn't actually want to 'go'. I would be walking a different way and it wasn't that far, but I didn't want to freak out again.

I spent ages putting the books away, turning my iPod off and winding the headphones carefully around it. I made sure my phone was in my right-hand jacket pocket so I could reach for it if I needed to. 'I want to go to taekwondo. I want to go to taekwondo,' I repeated in my head until I found myself outside the hall and breathed a sigh of relief. I was knackered already as I think I must have looked like one of those weird speed walkers considering how quickly I got there.

I had so much fun. It was amazing. There was a small group of us and we had such a laugh. I learnt loads and just having a workout and focusing on something different made me feel a million per cent better. Jane would roll her eyes at me if she heard me say that. 'You don't mean one million per cent, do you?' she'd say, and she would start her very boring lecture about percentages. I felt better anyway and I didn't think twice about walking home.

I wished I hadn't come home.

By the look on Mum's face, she had definitely forgotten about my early training session. Sammy was sitting in MY kitchen playing with MY dog.

'Hi, you're home, I wasn't expecting you until later,' she said in a slightly high-pitched tone.

I replied, 'Clearly.'

Sammy said, 'Hi, it's nice to see you again.'

'I'm going upstairs,' was all I could manage.

Reggie followed me as I left, which was good, because if he had chosen to stay with Sammy I might have cried. Looking at the perfect little 'happy family' scene downstairs, I don't think it's the first time they've met.

Reggie lay on my bed while I had a shower and got changed, then looked at me with his big, brown eyes and his super-cute head tilt as if to say, 'I don't like him really, I was just being nice.

I mean come on, the guy gave me some of his biscuit, what's a dog to do?' I should probably stop making up conversations with Reggie in my head. I'm sure it's a sign of madness.

'Did you have to be so rude?' Mum spat at me as she appeared at my bedroom door. Even Reggie looked like he knew this wasn't going to be fun. 'You've met Sammy before, he was only dropping me off after a meeting and came in for a cuppa. You could have been polite.' Before I even had a chance to reply she started talking again. Apparently I'm rude and selfish and I embarrassed her. I need to stop behaving like a spoilt brat as Sammy is sticking around even though… 'I wouldn't blame him for not wanting to stick around if you're going to keep behaving like that.'

The good thing was, I didn't even have to reply because she kept going on and on until she just turned and walked away with her parting shot. 'And you can cook your own dinner.' I tried not to laugh, but it looks like I'll be having toast tonight. I'm starving too.

I can hear that Mum is making her own dinner in the kitchen so there's no way I'm going downstairs yet. Reggie, the traitor, went running off downstairs as soon as he heard the fridge door open. How's that for loyalty?

Argh, I'm starving!

Thirty-two

I've been spending a lot of time in my room. It got so bad that I even started to catch up on coursework, but now I'm mainly watching YouTube videos of cute dogs and wondering how long it would take to make Reggie an internet sensation. So far, I've taught him to roll over, to give me a high five and to beg, where he sits up on his back legs and looks seriously cute. I think we're going to need to do a bit more than that before he becomes a superstar.

Half term is supposed to be fun, but I'm just not in the mood. It has been a long time since I had to talk myself into getting out of bed, but I'm back in that dark place again. This time, I have Reggie and my iPad though so it's much less lonely. I have a really long list of things I need to get finished before I go back to Sixth Form. I have to train for my next grading. I'm supposed to be seeing Amie and, at the moment, it's just all too much.

I missed taekwondo this weekend. That's when I knew things weren't right. I wanted to go, but couldn't. The little voice in my head was saying, 'But you know you love going, you know you'll feel better for going, and you know you can do this.' I lay in bed and cried. I just couldn't go. Mum must have noticed I didn't go, but didn't say anything about it. She still hasn't really said anything at all.

We were supposed to be going to see Amie yesterday and I sent her a text saying I was sorry but I didn't feel well. Even though it's sort of true, it also felt like a massive lie, which has made me feel even worse.

When I said to Mum that I didn't feel well, I honestly didn't expect her to go without me. She said, 'I hope you feel better soon.' The next thing I heard was her getting Reggie's stuff together and driving off to see Amie and her mum without me.

I had a text from Amie saying, 'Missed u but soooooo happy I saw Reg x.'

Firstly, his name is 'Reggie', not 'Reg', and secondly, I might as well not bother. If it's all about seeing him, then Mum can do what she likes with Amie and I can stay here. I don't need the hassle and have got loads to do. There are so many cute puppies on the internet I haven't seen yet, skateboarding dogs who need my attention and that's before I even get started on the other animals doing cute stuff.

What is it about Reggie that makes everything so much better? I know that he is the best thing that's ever happened to me, but how does he do this for everyone else too? He has some sort of magical power that just makes everything okay and makes the world a safe place to be. I don't know how he does it, but it seems to work for everyone.

It wouldn't have made any difference if I'd been there or not anyway because it's Reggie who helps Amie to feel better. It's he who can get her out the house and it's he who makes her laugh. It's stupid though because if I'd gone, he'd have done exactly the same thing for me. Then maybe we'd both have felt better.

I am supposed to be letting Frankie know about meeting up this week but haven't got back to her yet. I don't want her see me like this and I just don't think I've got the energy to pretend to be fine. I'm not fine. She was nice to me last week, but I know how boring it gets when your friends are miserable. I don't want to be miserable and definitely don't want to risk her not wanting to hang out with me anymore. If that happened, I think it would finish me. I really like hanging out with Frankie and really care about what she thinks. I told her that I had some training sessions for my next grading so that she didn't just think I was ignoring her. Another lie. What's happening to me? Am I now the sort of person who lies to people I care about?

I don't want to be this person.

Before Mum left for work, she took Reggie out and came up to tell me that she'd walked him. 'If you're feeling ill, it's one less thing for you to worry about,' she said. She then hit me with, 'If you need some time to think about the future and how you'd like it to be, Jane's said you can spend half term at her place.'

WHAT? So, they've been talking about all this, which is not surprise, but is it that bad that I might be getting sent to Jane's for some sort of intervention. Yep, I've been watching too much crap TV now I'm using words like 'intervention'. Seriously, like, do I need to go to Jane's like some sort of naughty kid being sent away to learn how to behave properly. I bet Mum just wants the place to herself to play happy families with Sammy and my dog. If I could take Reggie with me to Jane's then I might think about it, but there's no way I'm going there to be talked at for a week. No way. NO.

So much for a fun-filled half term. I'm lying under the duvet, with Reggie using the end of the bed for his personal washing area and I reckon there's more than enough videos I haven't watched yet to keep me occupied all day. I'm not thinking about everything else because it's just too hard at the moment.

Thirty-three

Apparently I have to get used to Sammy being around. Mum started off being nice about it all, tried to do things properly by letting us meet somewhere neutral and all that sort of stuff. Now, I think she's just fed up with me and I don't get a say in anything anymore.

I'm fed up with me too. I haven't left the house all week and I feel worse than I've felt in ages. I have had some messages with Frankie and Katie but haven't met up with them, I've missed taekwondo this week and the only thing I'm proud of is the fact I've finished a couple of pieces of coursework. I was too scared not to, because if I fail, I might have to do the whole year again. How embarrassing would that be? At least I could do the work without having to leave my room.

Mum sent me a text while she was at work this morning. 'Sammy is coming over for dinner. It will be on the table at 7pm, and you will be joining us.' I didn't even get a 'x'. A few weeks ago, I would have had a nice message about how it would mean a lot to her if I'd be there, that she would just like me to get to know Sammy, blah, blah, blah. Not anymore. Now, it's just an order to be in the kitchen at 7pm.

I got the message at about 11.30 in the morning, which was great because it meant I had almost a whole day to panic about it.

Seeing my friends was too much, going to taekwondo was too much, so how was I supposed to get through a dinner with Mum and Sammy. I like my friends, I love taekwondo, I don't like Sammy and right now, it's not like I'm getting on well with Mum either. I guessed that I'd have to get changed out my PJs too, which was asking a lot. The only reason I was getting changed was to take Reggie out and that was it.

I spent a lot of time wondering if it was worth just going to

Jane's for a couple of nights. I wondered if that was actually what Mum wanted me to do. Did she think I'd hate the idea so much that I'd just leave and then she could have a really nice evening without the hassle of me being there. I didn't want to go to Jane's, but I definitely didn't want to spend an evening with those two either. By about 1:30pm, I felt sick.

I sent Jane a message, 'Wud it be ok if I come and stay at urs 4 a couple of dayz? x'

'So your mum told you that you had to have dinner with her and Sammy then? x,' she replied.

What was I supposed to say to that? I didn't answer and just carried on panicking. About an hour later she sent another message:

'It'll be okay, take Reggie out, come home & have a shower, put on your favourite hoodie and go downstairs at 6.45pm. Make a drink for all of you and ask if you can help. Then, your mum will be happy & you'll have something to do. Good luck x.'

I cried.

I had plan, which was good, but I was still panicking. One step at a time, I still had a lot of time to kill before it was time for Reggie's walk. I didn't want to do any of those things, but my only other option was locking myself in my room. That was stupid as it would only make me look like more of an idiot, and there's no way Mum would have let me stay in my room without causing a scene. The mood she's in at the moment is a bit scary.

YouTube was the answer. The afternoon went really quickly, which was annoying. It never goes that quickly when I'm trying to get coursework done, or when I'm at Sixth Form. I went out with Reggie for an hour, and didn't give dinner a second thought. As usual, Reggie worked his magic and made me laugh while I was doing my best to keep him out of the pond. I thought that if I went home with a soggy, stinking dog, Mum would think I'd done it on purpose. A part of me that thought it would be funny, but was probably not the best idea I'd ever had.

We made it home without too much mud and a quick dry off was all he needed. While he started his post-walk washing routine, I started mine. I heard Mum's car pull up on to the drive and raced to the shower. Talking to her before dinner wasn't part of the plan and I couldn't deal with her nagging at me.

Showered, changed and ready. I had run out of excuses to stay upstairs so had to go downstairs. I went down to the kitchen, practicing what Jane had told me to do.

'Hi, would anyone like a drink?' I said as I walked into the kitchen. I forgot to wait for an answer before I then said, 'Can I help with anything?'

'Drinks would be perfect, thank you,' Mum said. I was given the order. I made drinks and sat with Reggie as they made small talk, asking me about taekwondo and how much coursework I had to do.

It wasn't as painful as it could have been. I was polite, I didn't say anything stupid and dinner was actually quite nice. It definitely made a change from toast, which is always good. Sammy was making an effort as usual, and I knew it was as crap for him as was for me. After dinner, I offered to sort out the dishwasher so that I didn't have to go and sit with them, but thankfully Sammy left soon afterwards.

I think Mum's still annoyed though because when I walked past the living room she just said, 'Thank you for tonight, I appreciate it.' That's all cool, but she didn't even look at me.

I'm back in bed, in my PJs, where I am planning to stay for most of tomorrow.

Thirty-four

Getting out of bed to go back to Sixth Form was hard this morning. It wasn't the normal 'I don't want to go to lessons' feeling, it was more than that. I didn't want to see people, I didn't want to have to make conversation and I didn't want to pretend to care about whatever we're supposed to be learning today. It was only the thought of failing and having to start all over again that got me out of bed. It didn't help that there was heavy rain and it was my morning to take Reggie out. It took me longer to dry him than it did to walk him; mainly because he thought the towel was there to play with and he turned it into a game of tug. At least one of us could just curl up in bed for the rest of the morning when all that was over. While Reggie made himself comfortable, I forced myself to get ready and leave the house.

Frankie met me for a hot chocolate before our first lesson. I wasn't looking forward to meeting up because I didn't want her to see me like this, but it was actually really nice. She made me laugh and for a few minutes, I didn't care about anything else. She spent a couple of days with her army friend over half term and was telling me how she had made an idiot out of herself, trying to prove she was as strong as everyone else. It turns out she wasn't that strong at all and fell off the tree she was trying to climb up. Luckily she walked away with only a couple of bruises but she said she was so embarrassed.

We were laughing as Katie joined us, but the laughter soon stopped as we had to listen to stories of how amazing her week was with her boyfriend, Cal. Seriously, why can't she just use his name? Frankie and I nodded in the right places and I tried hard not to laugh as Frankie rolled her eyes whenever Katie wasn't looking at her.

'My boyfriend Cal's going away for a couple of days so I thought we could have a girls' night at my place,' Kate said.

'Why does Cal, sorry, your boyfriend, Cal, have to be away for us to all get together?' asked Frankie, and immediately wished she hadn't.

'You'll understand when you meet someone special,' came the most patronising response ever from Katie.

I honestly thought Frankie was going to punch her as I cut in. 'That sounds good. When were you thinking of? I can bring some food.' All in an effort to try to calm things down. I then had my own reason to want to punch Katie as I added, 'It'll be nice to get away from Mum and her desperate need to try and get Sammy and me to be friends.'

Katie didn't even try to hide that she was rolling her eyes. 'Can't you shut up about your mum and Sammy? She just wants to be happy and I thought you said he was a nice guy? You're only allowed to come over if you don't talk about him.'

What was I supposed to say to that? The way I'm feeling at the moment, I'm surprised I didn't just burst into tears.

'I'll text you when I've sorted things with Mum,' Katie said as she walked away. She didn't seem to notice that neither of us said goodbye and that Frankie had quite a scary look on her face. I was glad I hadn't annoyed Frankie as even though she might not be great at tree climbing, I wouldn't want to put her strength to the test.

'How dare she say that to you?' Frankie said, once Katie was out of sight. 'Mate, I know it's hard with Sammy and you can talk about it as much as you like. If Katie won't listen because she's too wrapped up in her own sad little relationship, that's not friendship. I'm here, anytime.'

Then I really could have cried. I almost did and Frankie must have seen it as she put her arm around me and said, 'Come on, loser, it's time to go.'

I don't know how she does it but she made me laugh, she made me feel safe and for the first time in ages, I felt happy.

The day didn't go too badly after that. I got some results back and even though I know I can do better, I'm not failing. It's annoying because as soon as I saw the grades, I felt motivated to work harder. I know I can do better.

Now that I'm back home, sitting in my room with a whole evening free to do the work, I can't motivate myself. I had a text from Katie about the girls' night. I'm going to go, but only because Frankie is going. It'll be nice to see everyone and if I don't go, I'll only be sitting in my room feeling lonely. I obviously won't dare to talk about Sammy, but I bet I'll have to spend most of the night listened to stories about Cal. I might take bets on how long it takes Frankie to punch Katie. That will keep us all entertained!

I think Katie said that she'd be getting some films for us, so hopefully we'll have a break from her stories while the film is on. It's about all I have to look forward to at the moment, so I'm going to go, not think about anything else, and just try and be 'normal' for the night. It'll be fun, I hope.

Thirty-five

I'm in my room. I'm not leaving and I don't know what to do.

I went to Katie's last night. Everything was great, especially after what she had said earlier this week. Frankie was chilled and I wasn't even thinking about Sammy so definitely wasn't talking about him. Even Katie was back to her old self and having a laugh without constantly talking about Cal. It was amazing to have everyone together again. Callie was making us laugh as she had to race out and get nappy rash cream. She said it was the best way to help her new tattoo heal. That sounded pretty disgusting to me, and Frankie was convinced she got the tattoo just to save her the embarrassment of having to buy nappy rash cream because she actually had a nappy rash. Everything was great; we laughed, caught up on what's been happening and I got to play with Bailey, who loved me the most because I was the only one who remembered to being some treats for him as well as food for us.

Then it all went wrong. I didn't think to ask about what film we were watching. Why would I? When we're at home, Mum still double checks if there's a programme that I might not want to watch, she switches off the news sometimes if she hears me coming downstairs and we don't often watch films together. I had taken that for granted.

I got comfortable on the sofa with Bailey, Katie turned the lights off, told us all to shut up (in a nice way – sort of!) and the film started.

Who would choose to watch a film where girls are being raped and murdered? The opening scene made me feel sick. I was frozen to my seat on the sofa and if it wasn't for Bailey, I don't know what I would have done. For one hundred and twenty-seven minutes I tried to focus on stroking Bailey, on his breathing and on the fact I was safe, in Katie's house and my heart rate would go back to normal as soon as the film ended. It didn't.

I wasn't looking at the TV, I was looking at Bailey. That didn't take away the sound. Luckily, because the lights were off, I don't think anybody noticed my eyes were looking down. Because Katie had the volume up so loud, nobody could hear me desperately trying to control my breathing. I didn't cry, despite wanting to, I wasn't sick and that's a miracle. It was the longest one hundred and twenty-seven minutes of my life. Almost.

'Are you okay?' Frankie asked as the lights came back up.

'Yeah, all good but Bailey is squashing my legs and I need a wee!' I said, and I raced up to the bathroom.

'You could have moved the dog,' shouted Katie. She hopefully thought my run to the bathroom was because I needed a wee and not because I wasn't sure if I was going to be sick or not.

I could hear them talking as I was in the bathroom. 'That was pretty full on, shall we watch something funny next?'

'Pretty full on?' I couldn't believe that they could all watch something like that and just forget about it. I wish I could forget. I was relieved that they were choosing another film though because that meant I could lie on the sofa and not have to talk to anyone. I went back into the living room and the next film was just starting.

'Switch the lights off, Dan,' Frankie said as I walked back in.

Nobody noticed I was shaking as I crawled into my sleeping bag on the sofa and desperately tried to focus on the new film.

I heard Katie whisper, 'Maya, are you asleep.' Everyone started laughing. Maya was snoring! She was on a camp bed near my sofa and I think she'd been asleep for a while. I pretended to be asleep too as I heard the others go off to the kitchen to make drinks before heading upstairs. I heard them laughing and messing around, but I just couldn't go and join them. I wanted to go home but I was pretty sure Sammy would be there. I cried.

I couldn't sleep because every time I closed my eyes the images from the opening scene appeared. I couldn't get the sounds out of my head. I automatically started to think about what had happened to me. It was the longest night of my life, and when I heard my alarm go off this morning, I was relieved. Maya was still asleep so I quietly packed my things and left. They knew I'd be leaving early because I had taekwondo, so I sent Katie a text saying thanks and left a note saying I'd let Bailey out for a wee and that the keys were now through the front door.

I didn't go to taekwondo. I came straight home. Mum and Reggie are out; I guess with Sammy. I wish Reggie was here but I am glad Mum's out and I'm definitely glad I don't have to try and make an effort with Sammy. I'm knackered but I can't sleep, I'm hungry but I feel sick, I'm cold, even though I am under my duvet. Nothing makes sense. I don't know what to do. I can't ask Mum to come home because things still aren't great with us and I don't know what I'd say to her anyway. I don't want to talk to Jane, but only because I don't want to talk to anybody. Even with my music on, I can hear the sounds from the film. And even with my eyes open, I can see the opening scene. When I try to think about something else, all I can think of is what happened to me. I don't know what to do.

Thirty-six

I've told Mum I'm sick. I've spent the weekend in my room and she said that if I'm still sick tomorrow, she's taking me to the doctors. 'You can't miss Sixth Form without a doctor's note and if you're poorly again, we need to get you checked out,' she said.

I know that she doesn't believe me, which is okay because even though I feel like crap, I'm not actually sick.

If I don't get some sleep soon, I think I will be sick though. Every time I've tried to sleep, tried to think about something else, and tried to relax, it's been even worse. The sounds and the pictures won't go away. I've fallen asleep a couple of times, but I've woken up thanks to horrible nightmares. I can remember them; it's him, he's in my nightmares. I know that he's in prison and I know I'm safe at home, but that doesn't help when he appears in my nightmare and nothing makes sense. It's like that film opened a door in my mind and I don't know how to close it. The harder I try, the harder it is to focus on something else.

When it happened, Jane told me to break everything down into easy tasks, minute by minute, hour by hour, day by day. I'm too tired to try. Since I got home yesterday morning, I have been in my room with only a couple of quick trips to the bathroom. Mum has brought me tea and toast, which is apparently what you're supposed to have when you're ill, or when something bad has happened. I remember being offered a lot of tea and toast after it happened. Reggie is very happy with the appearance of toast but prefers Mum's toast as it has loads of butter on it. Mine doesn't. He comes upstairs, watches me eat mine and then has the crusts. He doesn't even look back towards me before he races down the stairs to find out if Mum has saved him some of hers. She always does. That boy has no loyalty when there's a possibility of food.

I even did some work this morning, that's how desperate I was to try to think about something else. It did help for a few minutes, but I was so tired, my eyes were closing as I was reading. I was too scared to fall asleep so started watching something on the laptop. It's still on in the background while I'm writing this, it's a film about two friends who are trying to change the world. One of them just asked the other to list five things she's grateful for. It's like Jane is now appearing in films to send me messages! Okay, I'll do my lists and see what happens. Maybe I can start by trying to feel better without having to leave my room. That sounds like a good plan to me.

I'm going to start with the things I'm grateful for, as that's the thing that Jane says works the best make people feel better.

What am I grateful for?

- Mum not questioning me too much about being sick.
- Reggie coming up to my room to lie with me, and Mum not sending him back downstairs. She still tries to keep the rule about him not being up here, which she knows is stupid.
- Despite the horrible film, I am grateful that I was invited to Katie's and that I have some friends to hang out with.
- I'm grateful it's the weekend so it doesn't matter if I spend the whole time in bed.
- I'm grateful that Frankie has been messaging me. She asked if she could come over but I told her I'd caught a bug and didn't want to make her sick too. Another lie, but I think it's better that way.
- I'm grateful for tea and toast being delivered to me.

That's actually quite a lot!

- Oh, and I'm definitely grateful for my bed, and my laptop.

I feel bad that I haven't been able to take Reggie out, so I'm grateful to Mum for doing that too.

What next? Success? That's a bit of a joke at the moment. My only success this weekend is writing this. It is not much to show for a weekend at home. I can't really think about any big goals either. I still want all of the things I've always wanted. I want to work towards my black belt, I want to pass my A Levels and I want to do something useful with my life. Right now though, I can't think past getting some sleep and maybe making it to the kitchen so that I can have something to eat that isn't toast. When it happened and I couldn't sleep, Mum used to make me hot milk and sit with me, just like she did when I was little. She's sit there and wait until I'd fallen asleep, and I think in the early days, she'd just sleep in the chair next to my bed. Sometimes I'd wake up and she'd still be there. I don't want her to sit with me, too much has changed and I want to figure this out myself, but I do now want to have some warm milk!

That's my goal. I'm going to get up out of bed, go downstairs to the kitchen, play with Reggie for a few minutes and then come back upstairs with some hot milk, like a proper big kid. I don't care, Mum's out and I know that Reggie won't tell anyone. He can come and sit with me so that if I fall asleep, I'll definitely feel safer. I bet Frankie would call me a loser if she knew this was going to be the best part of my weekend. Maybe she'd just laugh with that little smile she gives me when she knows something is wrong, but also knows I don't want to talk about it. Right, I'm going downstairs!

Thirty-seven

I'm being sent to therapy boot camp. That's what it feels like anyway. I'm supposed to be up here packing but I just want to cry. Again.

I refused to go to the doctors this morning. Mum came up and said that if I was still poorly, I needed to go. I know that I don't need a doctor, I just need some sleep.

'You can't carry on like this, Danielle,' she had added

Uh oh, I knew it was going to turn into a full-blown lecture because she called me 'Danielle'. To be fair, she's called me 'Danielle' a lot recently.

I rolled over in bed and said, 'I'll be fine tomorrow, just leave me alone.'

'You know I'm not going to leave you alone,' she said in a much softer voice. 'Please tell me what's going on with you, I'm worried.'

That was enough for the tears to start falling. I couldn't help it. It was the first time in ages Mum had been nice to me. She'd probably disagree with that, but that's what it felt like. Everything came spilling out of my mouth. Not just the film...everything.

I told her about how scared I was of having a Sammy in the house, about the guy who I thought was following me, and about the film night at Katie's. I told her that I was having nightmares, and that I couldn't stop seeing the images or hearing the sounds and that I had no control over it.

'I used to be able to think about what happened to me,' I said. 'And then move on to think about something else, something better. Now, I haven't got any control over it and it's frightening.' My eyes wouldn't stop leaking, there was even stuff coming out of my nose. I hadn't cried like that in ages. It was disgusting and a relief all at the same time.

Mum sat and listened. She didn't ask me anything, didn't say anything and she just let me talk. I'm pretty sure that most of what I was saying didn't make any sense, so maybe she couldn't understand the words, but I didn't stop talking for ages.

'Oh, Dani, I had no idea,' came her words of wisdom when I'd stopped to take a breath. At least she wasn't calling me 'Danielle' anymore, so that was progress. I kept crying and she rubbed my arm saying, 'It's okay, we'll get this sorted.'

The next thing I remember was her knocking on my door with – guess what? Yes, tea and bloody toast. Seriously, I'm going to turn into a piece of toast at this rate.

I must have cried myself to sleep as it was lunchtime when she woke me up. 'What's happening?' I asked, as there's no way she should be at home on a Monday. 'Why aren't you at work?'

'I've taken a couple of days off. I've called your Sixth Form and said you've got a bug so you won't be in this week and tomorrow we're going to Jane's.'

So, basically, I get to spend today feeling sorry for myself and tomorrow, it's boot camp. Mum is driving me to Jane's and we're spending the day there. Then, Mum is driving home and leaving me at Jane's for the rest of the week. I don't get a say in it at all. I tried to argue, saying that I'd miss taekwondo and that I had loads of work that was due in.

But Mum was ready for that. 'You haven't been to taekwondo recently so another week won't hurt and I have arranged for an extension on your deadlines,' she said. 'Jane'll make sure you've got time and space to do your work and you can practice taekwondo there too.'

'What about Reggie?' I didn't want to go and spend a week without him. He's the only thing keeping me sane at the moment although after this morning's waterfall, Mum might disagree with that.

'Danielle, you haven't been walking him recently and he'll be just fine for a few days with me.'

That hurt. She's right, but that hurt. She can use my full name all she likes but throwing it in my face that I haven't been doing my best for Reggie really hurt.

So here I am, avoiding packing, a failure on every level.

Mum must have put my phone on silent when I was asleep because I've just seen messages from Frankie. 'R u okay, dude? X,' was the last one, after the usual jokes about me being late.

I replied saying I'd be back next week. 'Dox orderz x.' Jane is a doctor, after all. She's not a real one, but that doesn't seem to matter.

'Miss ya x,' she wrote back and that made my eyes leak again.

I miss Frankie too. She's the best thing that's happened to me, especially since Katie has ditched us all for the romance of the century and Callie is off having arty adventures and Maya is always doing something musical. If it wasn't for Frankie, things would be a lot worse right now.

I can't help wondering if part of the reason I am being sent to Jane's is so that Mum can have Sammy here. I wouldn't dare say that to her at the moment, but I've never been sent to Jane's before. I'll be out of Mum's way, she won't have to give me a second thought and she can have a great time here with Sammy. Maybe I'm just being a bitch. Jane's taken some time off work so that I can go and stay, but why couldn't she come here. Mum said a change of scenery would do me good. Will it? Me not being here might do her good? She'll kill me if I said that out loud.

Reggie got excited when he saw me get the big bag out of the wardrobe. I hope that's because he thinks he's going on an adventure and not because he's excited I'll be leaving for a few days. I can't believe I'm even thinking that. I definitely need some more sleep.

Thirty-eight

Day one of boot camp is over. The drive here was a bit awkward with Mum making digs about me being on my phone. 'You could talk to me?'

That was Mum's epic conversation starter. What am I supposed to say to that?

'What d'you want to talk about?' I asked.

I got more annoyed when she replied, 'Anything.' What does that mean? Should I talk about world peace, Callie's new tattoo, or a video I saw on the internet? Otherwise, the things that she would probably like to talk about: why I'm so unhappy and how things can be great with me and Sammy.

I stuck to playing on my phone as that was the easiest way to get through the journey. Mum didn't stay too long because she said she wanted to get back for Reggie. I don't think that Reggie was the only guy she wanted to get back for, but at least he was on the list.

How long does it take for a dog to forget you? I'm going to be at Jane's until Friday evening, so that's three nights but almost four whole days. What if I go back and Reggie has forgotten me, or thinks I've left him and I don't care anymore? He doesn't know, does he? All he knows is that I was there, as usual, this morning and that Mum walked through the door, by herself, this afternoon. I wish that there was a way I could explain to him. I actually wish that right now I was in my own room, in my own bed and things were good again. Mum has sent me a couple of messages with pictures of Reggie. She took him to the park and now he's asleep by her feet as she's watching TV. I couldn't see Sammy in the picture, but I bet he's there.

Today hasn't been as bad as I thought it would be though. While Mum was still here, she was just catching up with Jane. Apparently there's someone who Jane has been on a couple of dates with so they were both really excited. I'm not sure if I was supposed to hear about it as they changed the subject when I came back in the room. Maybe it's just me being paranoid but I'm also quite pleased I don't have to listen to someone else talking about how amazing it is to be in a relationship.

'Look after my baby girl,' Mum had said as she left.

'You know I will,' I replied, before Jane could say anything.

'So, what happens now? Do I need to go and lie on a couch or get fitted for a straightjacket?' I asked Jane after she shut the door.

'I was thinking about taking you for a pub lunch, but I can lock you in a padded cell if you'd prefer,' came the reply.

That wasn't a difficult decision. 'As long as I can have something other than tea and toast, I'm happy.'

Lunch was great, not just because it didn't involve toast. It was nice to do something different, talk to someone different and not feel like I had to pretend everything was okay. I really do love my new friends, I'm happy at Sixth Form, especially compared to the living hell of secondary school, but I do feel under pressure to make sure people think I'm okay. With Jane, it was fine for me to sit quietly and spend ages trying to make a decision about what to eat. I have totally lost the ability to make decisions recently. She waited and when I was ready, went and ordered. She didn't mind that it took me a long time to eat, but did laugh at me when I was able to decide on a pudding much more quickly than I'd been able to decide on lunch. If there's a cheesecake on the menu, it's a pretty easy decision for me.

Walking home, I thanked Jane for lunch and for taking the time off work. 'I do appreciate it, I just wish we didn't have to do this,' I said.

'I'd rather you came to stay just because you wanted to see me,' she responded, and that surprised me. I'd never even considered the possibility that Jane actually might want to see me. She's always been really nice to me. She's been a huge part of my life and I love her like I do my own Mum, maybe more at the moment (!). But I thought I was just part of the 'package deal' because she was friends with Mum. Maybe I'm not. Maybe she actually likes me? Weird.

We haven't talked about much today and that's been a relief. After lunch, Jane said she needed to catch up on a little bit of work so that she could then switch off for the week. I watched some rubbish daytime television and Jane sent me out to get some milk.

'If you're anything like your Mother, you'll need milk for your ridiculous amounts of tea,' she'd said. Jane didn't have any milk in the house at all. What is wrong with her? She drinks a lot of black coffee, which stinks, and I definitely couldn't last nearly a whole week without a cuppa. Maybe I'm more like Mum than I thought.

While drinking 'ridiculous amounts of tea', which was actually only three cups, we spent the evening watching a funny film. We were both still full from lunch and it was nice just to do nothing. Jane hasn't said anything about getting my homework done, yet. I don't think I'll be able to go a whole week without her saying anything, but today has been like a little holiday.

I sent a goodnight text to Mum, not for her, for Reggie, and had a reply with a picture of him lying on his back with his legs in the air, sound asleep. He doesn't look like he's missing me as much as I'm missing him.

Thirty-nine

I might need that padded cell after all. Jane has made sure that it's not a holiday and I'm sooooo tired. I didn't think that talking could be this exhausting. I wasn't joking when I said I'd been sent to boot camp.

In a weird sort of way, I think feeling like this has been something that has been ready to happen for a while. There's been so much going on and I haven't been able to talk to anyone. I've been doing my best to do the things I want to do: taekwondo, getting through Sixth Form without failing, and spending time with my friends. I should have spotted that things were going wrong when I was making excuses and not taking Reggie out. Spending time with him is my most favourite thing to do. Once it also moved to missing taekwondo and then not wanting to see my friends, there was definitely something wrong. I can't pretend that wanting to miss Sixth Form is a sign that something is wrong as I don't know anyone who bounces out of bed excited to get to class, but it's not the worst place in the world.

Being at home used to be my safe place. I love our home and I especially love my little room. Since Mum met Sammy, it hasn't been the same. I've been so worried about him being there, or the scariest thing, that Mum might want him to move in, that it hasn't felt the same. Jane has told me that Mum needs to know how I feel. She thinks she's been good to me about Sammy, that she hasn't pushed me to spend too much time with him and that she's respecting our home by keeping it 'ours'. She has no idea about how I feel. Sammy has made an effort to be nice to me and I know that there's no reason to be scared, but my brain doesn't work logically about these things. Jane said that I might like Sammy if I got to know him a bit better and then see if I feel like I can trust him.

'Mum must have paid you to say that.' I laughed but I know it makes sense. Things quite often make sense when I'm with Jane, but then when I try to do something about it, it doesn't make sense any more.

While I'm sitting here, I feel happy about making an effort to get to know Sammy. I need to figure out how to keep feeling like this when I get home. I need to be able to tell Mum how I feel without her thinking I'm a spoilt bitch who doesn't want her to be happy.

'I'm not talking to her on your behalf. You're more than grown up enough to be able to talk to her,' Jane said in support, after I asked her if she'd talk to Mum for me.

Nice. I'm going home tomorrow so I need to get myself ready for the conversation.

I had my first proper night's sleep last night too. I can't remember the last time I slept properly. I didn't have a nightmare and that was amazing.

I talked to Jane about the film, about how I felt I had to sit through it so that the girls didn't think I was a loser and how I wanted to be normal, like them.

She laughed at the fact I called my friends 'normal'. 'Explain to me how a group of girls is normal?' she asked. 'They're so different, they'll annoy you sometimes, they'll have things they're frightened of, and all have secrets, too. So, you're perfectly normal, if that's what you're aiming for.' Okay, so she has a point. She finished with, 'D'you think they'd be happy with you calling them normal?'

Okay, Jane has me there. Callie would be offended, Frankie would definitely be offended, Maya is too laid back to care and Katie would be insulted as she thinks she's way better than 'normal'. They're not normal at all. They're all way too awesome to be normal. Even Katie who is seriously doing my head in most of the time. They all have things that they're frightened of, even if I don't know about them. I don't think I'd be too happy if they described me as 'normal' either, now that I'm thinking about it.

I'm supposed to be getting ready to go out for dinner, not writing in my diary. Jane can't say anything though because I've promised I'll go back to writing in here like I used to. We're going out with the woman she's been on a few dates with. She asked me if I wanted to go.

'No, not really,' I said as I was hoping to have a final night of chilling out before going home to face the music.

'She's a black belt in taekwondo,' Jane replied.

'Yes, I'll be ready. What time? She sounds amazing.'

I'm quite easily impressed apparently. She can't be an idiot if she has her black belt.

'If Sammy had a black belt maybe I'd have liked him from the start,' I said to Jane, half-joking.

So, before I go and annoy this poor woman with thousands of questions, I need to do this:

Goals

- It's May and I have my red belt in taekwondo – *the April deadline has slipped a bit, but that's okay.*
- By the end of this weekend, I'll have my three assignments finished – *thanks to being at boot camp, I've already done most of them. One of them Jane helped with so I'd better get a good grade.*
- I have walked Reggie every day for a month – *this is the one thing that I need back in my life as soon as I'm home. Walking him is amazing as we have a laugh together, but it also means I have to leave the house and get some exercise and fresh air. Once I'm back in the routine, it'll be fine.*

Success

- I slept through the night – *I sound like a baby!*
- I've talked to Jane about things – *which is a success to me as last week I couldn't imagine talking to anyone about anything.*

- I've done a lot of work to make sure I'm (nearly) up to date with assignments.
- I've practiced my taekwondo moves every day – *I can't wait to get back to training on Saturday.*

Gratitude

- I am grateful to Jane; she didn't have to take time off to help me. I am glad she did.
- I'm grateful to Mum for lying for me! I haven't had to worry about Sixth Form or what my friends think. I can go back next week and just say I feel better, which is true.
- I'm grateful to Frankie for keeping in touch and sending me 'get well' messages. I have heard from Katie too, once, which to be fair, was amazing as she didn't mention Cal, her boyfriend!

Forty

The journey home was a lot better than the journey here on Tuesday. Mum brought Reggie to come and pick me up. Jane wasn't thrilled as he was bouncing all around her kitchen but I could have cried at how excited he was to see me. I think I've run out of tears, so instead, I went to take him for a walk while Mum and Jane talked.

'Tell Mum all about Lucy,' I said as Reggie dragged me out of the front door. 'OMG, she's seriously awesome.'

It's true, she really is awesome. I had the best night, and felt sorry for Jane because she didn't really get to talk to Lucy at all. They haven't been seeing each other very long, but Jane said she thought Lucy would help motivate me to carry on with taekwondo. She definitely did that. Lucy still trains every week and is now going to be an instructor. She said I could train with her next time I'm staying with Jane, if I want to. Of course I want to!

'So, you approve of Lucy then?' Jane asked as we walked back into her house.

'She's amazing,' I said, and meant it.

It's nice that Jane's with someone and is happy.

Mum started to pack up the car and Jane whispered, 'It was just dinner, and a chat to get to know someone. There's no reason why you couldn't do that with Sammy too.'

Why does everything have to come with a lecture when I'm with Jane?

'That's true, but I haven't got anything in common with Sammy,' I argued.

'You both like your mum,' was her stupid response to that. Great so I can start with that when I go and make an effort with Sammy, that's helpful.

Being out with Reggie was the best end to my boot camp. I

was sad to say goodbye to Jane, but so pleased I was reunited with my favourite boy, I couldn't wait to leave. I have learnt that it takes more than four days for a dog to forget about you, so that's a relief.

'You're sounding more like Jane than ever,' Mum said, after I told her about how amazing the evening with Lucy was. 'So, you'll be going back to taekwondo tomorrow?' she added.

'Can't wait to get back into it all,' I replied. 'I want to train harder than ever.'

'I have a plan for us tomorrow when you're back, just you, me and Reggie.' I decided not to interrupt her by asking what it was while she was in full flow. '...Then on Sunday, we're booked in with Amie, if that's okay?'

I'm looking forward to seeing Amie actually. I feel like I've been letting her down because I've felt rubbish, so it'll be good to see her and find out how she's doing.

I thought Mum was going to crash the car when I said, 'I'll need a little bit of time to finish my assignments too.'

Mum collected a takeaway on the way home, which sent Reggie into excitement overdrive in the back of the car. He was disappointed when we got home and he found out it wasn't for him. He looked to me, then to Mum, then back to me hundreds of times while we ate. He does the most amazing 'please feed me' face which I find very hard to resist. I saved him some chicken and rice, which he inhaled, and then went to focus on what Mum had left. Once again, his loyalty was very much food related.

After Reggie had double-checked every inch of the carpet in the hope that we'd dropped a grain of rice, he settled down by my side, took a deep breath and slept soundly for the rest of the evening.

'He missed you,' Mum assured me. 'He was looking for you at first, checking your room and looking around the house.'

That made me happy and sad at the same time. I was pleased

that he cared enough to notice, but then felt bad that he was upset.

'He'll be very happy you're home now, and so am I,' Mum added.

'It's nice to be home,' I said, and I meant it. It does feel good to be home. While everything was relaxed, I forced out, 'I'll make more effort with Sammy.' I know that I should probably tell Mum how I'm feeling but I'm so tired from all the talking with Jane, I just wanted to relax.

'I'd appreciate that, and so would Sammy. He's a nice guy and I think if you get to know him, you'd like him too.'

Maybe it's that simple. Maybe if I just try to get to know him, like Jane said, then I'll feel safer about him being around. Mum's going to arrange something so we can go out for dinner. I'm happy about that as we can start over.

It's really nice to be back in my own bed!

Forty-one

I probably won't be telling my friends about today, but I've had a really good day.

The first amazing thing was that I slept really well and didn't have a nightmare. Well, if I did, I don't remember it which is good enough for me. It was brilliant to be back in my own room but I was a bit scared the same thing would happen again. My alarm went off so that I could eat and get ready for training and it was a little while before I even realised that everything was okay. That's got to be a good sign that I'm feeling better.

Taekwondo was tough. My body didn't like it but my brain was loving it. Taking some time off hasn't helped my fitness at all and I noticed that I was slower in some of the moves. That's a lesson for me about making sure I don't miss sessions like I've done these past few weeks. I'll never get my black belt if I carry on like this. I'm really sore now, but it's quite a nice ache. It means I've done something positive and worked my body.

I'm pleased with myself for going even though I was a bit nervous when I walked in. Everyone was really nice, they asked how I was and asked if I was feeling better, then we got on with the session. One of the things I love about this group is that everyone is there for the same reason and there's no drama. Once I said I was feeling better and thanked them for asking, that was it, we started to warm up and everything was back to normal.

My instructor said that I had some work to do if I was aiming to go for my next grading in May. 'It's doable, if you want it badly enough,' he said. It was all he needed to say to get me working hard. I really do want it. Badly.

Next came Mum's plan for an afternoon out. When I got home, she was waiting with a picnic box and Reggie was much more excited than usual. Mum said that was because he'd seen sausage rolls go into the picnic box and he wasn't sure what he needed to do in order for her to take them out again. I bet he was really just waiting for her to leave the kitchen so that he could break into the box and eat the lot.

'Get yourself ready as quick as you can, Reggie is going to explode if he doesn't get a sausage roll soon,' Mum shouted up the stairs as I raced to the shower. Who am I to prevent my best friend from having his sausage roll?

'I've entered Reggie into a charity dog show,' Mum said as we got into the car.

'Seriously? He's going to win everything. What are the categories?'

I probably should have asked about the categories before claiming he'd win everything, as he didn't stand a chance in 'Prettiest Bitch'. That is an actual category. I took a photo and sent it to Frankie saying, 'I've entered you into a competition.'

She replied saying she was already the National Champion, which made me laugh.

'You're sounding happier, are you pleased you went to Jane's?' Mum asked as I made an effort and put my phone away.

'Yeah, it was nice to have some time out and get my head together. It was really nice to meet Lucy too.'

Mum jumped on that and said, 'Well, speaking of relationships, would you like to come out for dinner with Sammy tomorrow after we've seen Amie?'

I'm pretty sure we weren't talking about relationships, but I just said, 'Sure, where're we going?' I carried on reading the event list while Mum had a conversation with herself about which pub she'd rather go to. 'Anywhere with cheesecake is good with me,' I chipped in, but I don't think she was listening.

Reggie was a superstar at the dog show. It was a charity thing for a local rescue centre and we found out that in a few weeks there's another show for the rescue centre Reggie came from. 'I'd love to take him so that they can see how happy he is,' I said to Mum.

'Do you think he'll get upset and think we're taking him back,' she replied.

One of the volunteers overheard us and Mum got really embarrassed when he said, 'Don't worry, it's at a local community farm, not at the rescue centre itself so he'll be just fine.'

Walking away, Mum reassured me. 'I was only joking.' But I wasn't convinced, and nor was the man volunteering.

We walked away with first prize in the 'Most Handsome Male' category and third prize in the 'Best Trick' category. Obviously, the 'most handsome male' was going to go to Reggie, that was never in question and I'm definitely not biased. I was really pleased with the third place too and I think Mum might actually have cried.

When we first tried, Reggie got a little bit distracted and tried to get one of the other dogs to play with him. Luckily he came back and we did our whole repertoire of tricks (only four, but that's not bad for beginners) and he was amazing. First place went to a guy who pretended to shoot his Jack Russell and the cute little dog did the best acting I've ever seen. He literally jumped, fell backwards and lay still until the guy called him. We couldn't compete with that, but next year, we're going for the win. I'm not sure Reggie's got the competitive edge he needs as he was playing with the Jack Russell as soon as he could and even shared his third place treats. So cute.

I'm now up in my room while Mum's on the phone to Sammy sorting out tomorrow's dinner plans. I'm feeling all right about it all at the moment and am looking forward to seeing Amie tomorrow too. It's amazing what a difference a week makes.

Forty-two

Today has been mixed, but on the positive side, if this had happened a couple of weeks ago I'd probably have had a complete meltdown and not been able to cope at all.

Check me out looking for the positives, Jane would be impressed.

After a walk in the sun with Reggie, I was feeling really good and excited about seeing Amie. Reggie was all set for his day out and Mum was already talking about how excited she was about dinner later.

All was well, until we got to Amie's house, knocked on the door and Nina was there. I haven't seen her for ages and the second I saw her, I felt like crap. The Queen Bully of my horrible year at the local secondary school was looking at me and was about as pleased to see me as I was to see her.

'Hey, Amie's upstairs,' she said. I'll go and get her.' She turned and walked up the stairs.

I was holding on to Reggie's lead and hadn't realised I'd been holding on tight. He was standing next to me, really still and his tail wasn't wagging. 'It's okay, puppy power, nobody likes her but remember we're here to be nice to Amie,' I whispered, and I knelt down beside him. His tail started wagging again and he was definitely much happier when he saw Amie appear at the top of the stairs.

My heart rate returned to normal as Mum said, 'It's such a nice day, we've brought some food so why don't we head straight out to the park?' I was so relieved. Seeing Nina was a surprise I didn't need just as things were starting to get better. It's not like she's done anything to me since I'd started meeting up with Amie but it doesn't change the fact she made my life a complete misery.

Amie raced out to greet Reggie and along with her mum and

another bag of food, we all climbed into the car.

'Nina said she didn't want to come with us,' Amie revealed as we drove away.

I saw Mum looking at me in the mirror and I managed to say, 'That's cool, there's no room in the car anyway.' Which was about as relaxed as I was able to be. I don't think Nina would ever choose to spend the day with us, but even the thought that she might, sent me into a minor panic.

Amie's mum changed the subject, asking me if I was feeling better and how Sixth Form was going. Nina wasn't mentioned again and by the time we'd got to the park, I had decided to just be pleased with myself for not totally freaking out.

It was a good day. Amie was doing really well, was back at school and was excited to tell me that she was sort of seeing a guy at her school. 'It's really early days and he's really relaxed so we're just hanging out at the moment.'

She sounded really grown up and for a moment I felt like the kid. Everyone around me was starting relationships and for me, it has just never happened. How could Amie be so relaxed about it?

'It's just like having a really good friend whom you also want to kiss,' she added, which is probably the best explanation I've ever heard.

I told her about Katie and how she'd become obsessed with her boyfriend and asked her not to get like that.

'She's being a total loser,' said Amie. Her insightful comments just flowed as if she was the older, wiser person in the discussion.

'A friend whom you also want to kiss.' Maybe that did make a lot of sense.

Reggie stopped that thought developing by running up to us and dropping his soggy tennis ball in Amie's packet of crisps. He couldn't have timed that any better. She was not happy, and even less happy when he then stuck his giant dripping wet nose in the packet of crisps because he wanted to play and she was too slow in throwing the ball. Out came the tennis ball and he ran off to entertain himself while Amie sulked because there weren't any more crisps she could have. Maybe she's not the grown up after all!

Back home, with a tired Reggie, all I wanted to do was go and lie on the sofa. I had a text from Jane wishing me luck for tonight and thought I'd feel more awake and ready to make an effort after a shower. By the time we got to the pub, I was so hungry that I'd almost forgotten I also had to be nice to Sammy. Because we'd been so busy, I didn't have time to worry about dinner and I think that helped. I tried to see Sammy as Mum's friend, thanks to Amie's wisdom. We actually had a bit of a laugh and he was impressed that Reggie came third in the tricks. He said he had a friend who could help us teach Reggie the 'shooting' trick, so maybe he could be useful after all. I'm not sure what he meant by 'us', but I'll worry about that another day.

Tonight, I am feeling quite proud of myself. A text from Jane made me smile too. 'I hear tonight went really well, I'm proud of you x.' Well done me!

What can I succeed at next while I'm on a roll?

Goals

- It's May and I have my red belt in taekwondo – *I'm practicing.*
- By the end of this weekend, I'll have my three assignments finished – *done! There'll be loads to catch up on after my week off, but these three are finished.*
- I have walked Reggie every day for a month – *so far so good.*

Success

- I didn't freak out when Nina opened the door.
- I was nice to Sammy and actually had an okay evening.

- I've done my assignments and can hand them in tomorrow morning.

Gratitude

- I am grateful for Amie; it was so good to see her doing well today.
- Yesterday's dog show was a lot more fun than I thought it would be and I'm grateful to have the most amazing dog, ever.
- I'm grateful that the sun was shining today so I didn't have to stay in the house with Nina!

Forty-three

I haven't written for a few days because I've been way too busy. I know that Jane wouldn't be impressed with me for saying that but I don't care because I'm feeling really good. This has been the best Easter Break and I'm even looking forward to going back to Sixth Form next week.

I have my red belt. I actually have it. I can't believe it. After the last couple of months, I honestly didn't think I'd do this and I'm so happy. I've worked really hard since getting back from Jane's. Meeting Lucy was a push in the right direction too and getting back to taekwondo has helped my head as well as my body. It didn't take long for me to feel strong again, and I proved that today.

'Focus and hard work, you did yourself proud today,' my instructor had said as he handed me my belt and certificate. I felt happier than I've felt in months.

I'd turned around to see Mum wiping away a tear as she'd mouthed, 'Well done, love.'

See, when I put my mind to something, I really can do it. I just needed some help to kick-start me again.

Everyone else had soon joined in. 'Lucy says congratulations, and I'm really proud of you, x,' Jane messaged.

Another text came in from Frankie saying, 'Does this mean u get new pjs x'.

I think she meant 'Congratulations'! We're going out to celebrate later, which I'm really looking forward to. She's coming over soon so we can finish our assignment on nutrition for performance sport. There's a kind of irony that we're then going to go out and eat pizza.

I have been looking forward to tonight almost as much as getting through my grading. I feel like I was a rubbish friend when I was in the dark place. I know I was a rubbish friend. I missed Frankie, but I also didn't want her to see me in such a bad way. I don't think she would have cared, but it matters to me that she doesn't think I'm an idiot. It matters more than it has mattered with my other friends.

I've tidied up so that we can get through the assignment as quickly as possible and then head out for food. Last time Frankie was here, she spent more time messing around with Reggie than she did trying to get anything done. He was happy with that and will probably be very happy to see her. Almost as happy as me.

He should be tired, but it doesn't take much to wake him up again. We've been practicing some more tricks so that we can try and win the next dog show. It's not like I can make him any more handsome and I reckon he'll win that again, easily! We're not very good at the moment and Sammy has tried to help since he asked his friend about it.

We had quite a good evening last week. Sammy came over for dinner and brought a video link to help with the shooting trick. He tried to let me get on with it, but couldn't help getting involved. The good thing was that Reggie was much more responsive to me, even though Sammy had obviously watched the video loads of times to try to learn how to do it.

That's my boy. We're getting there, slowly. The thing with Reggie is that even when he's doing really well, once he goes to sleep, it's as if he forgets everything and we have to start from scratch again.

'You can't have exceptional brains and exceptional beauty,' was Sammy's way of trying to be funny.

'No, you definitely can't,' said Mum, a little bit too quickly, which made me laugh. I'm still not sure if that means she thinks that Sammy is a bit thick or not very good-looking.

Okay, to make sure I'm getting back on track, I need to do this before Frankie gets here:

Goals

- It's August and I have my new belt in taekwondo – *I'm*

getting much closer to my black belt.

- By the end of the holiday, I'll have all of my assignments finished – *I still have to do the nutrition one and I'll probably need to message Maya for some tips about the psychology one, but I'll worry about that tomorrow.*
- I will walk Reggie every day – *not only walking, we're practicing our tricks too. He's definitely helping to keep me focused. I have started to learn what it must be like for my taekwondo instructor when I just don't get what he's asking me to do. It's the same for me when I'm trying to teach Reggie and he's just looking at me but not moving.*

Success

- Red Belt. That is all!

Gratitude

- I am grateful for my taekwondo instructor for having the patience to help me get this far.
- I can't believe I'm going to write this but I'm grateful to Sammy for finding out about the trick stuff for Reggie.
- I'm grateful that I have the evening planned with Frankie.

Forty-four

After an awesome couple of days, my sanity was put to the test today. Some people really are too stupid and can't think past themselves.

Frankie and I were put into a group with another couple of people in class today. I haven't really spoken to Matt and Adam before and they're always making jokes through class and making excuses for not having finished assignments. I'm not completely sure how they haven't been thrown out. We were supposed to be talking about the differences between training for football and training for rugby, putting together some ideas about developing fitness and then talking about the impact of contact in sport. With both of these guys being rugby players, they decided to take over and, while I kept quiet, Frankie was trying to make it very clear that she knew as much as they did about the sports. This is where having a dad could have come in very useful as all of Frankie's knowledge came from sitting with her dad as he shouted at the television. The guys weren't impressed. It wasn't long before they were chatting about their next fixture and Frankie and I were attempting to get our heads around the differences.

We were going through the questions that we needed to answer when, out of nowhere, one of the guys, Matt, said, 'It'll be a thrashing, we'll rape them and they won't even see it coming.'

I froze. I literally froze. I looked down and stared at my feet, wondering if everyone could hear my heart beating as loudly as I could. I felt like the whole room had gone quiet and that everybody was staring at me. I took a breath, dared to look up and the room immediately came back into focus.

Frankie was still writing, Matt was laughing and Adam had already moved on to how he was going to go out afterwards and celebrate their win. As I carefully looked around the room, I could see that everybody else was chatting in their groups; nobody was looking at me and it seemed that nobody thought there was anything wrong with what he'd just said.

'You okay? Come on, stop daydreaming. I need help here,' said Frankie.

I was still looking around the room. Seriously, had nobody else heard that? 'I'm just going to the loo,' I replied. Once I was out of the room, I ran to the toilets.

This reminded me of last year. I was so scared of what Nina and her gang of giggling freaks would say that I would hide in the toilet and wait until the breaks were over. This was different. They had no idea that what they'd just said made me feel like that, it wasn't deliberate, but who would use that word? There are so many words they could use. Why that one? Adam had laughed as Matt said it. Do they have any idea what that word actually means? I'm sure they wouldn't be laughing if it happened to either of them. Do guys find it easier to joke about? I couldn't believe that Frankie didn't even look up when they said it. I guess she might not have heard it, but I think I would have picked that word out of any conversation that was happening in the room. It hit me so hard.

Sitting in a Sixth Form toilet is not the best place to try to calm down by taking deep breaths. I'm not sure if it was the deep breathing that made me feel sick, but I definitely felt rough. I needed to get back before it got weird. Racing out to the toilet in the middle of a lesson and being a long time would mean that there would have been jokes when I went back in. Walking back, I tried to be rational. They are idiots. They have no idea about the impact of their words. They are idiots. They will probably be thrown out of Sixth Form soon because they are idiots. They didn't deliberately try and hurt me. They are idiots.

I walked back in and sat down, focusing on Frankie and ignoring the idiots. They were talking about some new app they had on their phones and didn't notice I was back. They probably hadn't noticed I'd gone. They are idiots.

I helped Frankie write up some notes but said that I didn't want to present anything in front of the whole group. I was proud of myself for just being back in the room, I didn't want to try talking as well.

'Jeez, do I have to do everything.' She sighed as she stood up to present what we'd done. Well, what she had done.

'Nice job, thanks for doing that,' I whispered as she sat back down. She rolled her eyes at me, which meant I was forgiven.

Luckily, that was the final lesson of the day so I said goodbye and went to taekwondo. I did think about heading straight home but I definitely needed to punch something.

They really are idiots. I'm proud of myself though, I didn't have a total breakdown. Maybe one day I'll be strong enough to challenge them. I bet Amie would have done!

So, back to the good stuff now I'm home:

Goals

- It's August and I have my next belt in taekwondo – *I'm pleased that I went training tonight. If I'd missed it, I think it would have been a sign of me going back towards the dark place.*
- It's half term and I have handed in all of my assignments – *I am almost up to date at the moment. I might need to ask Frankie to remind me about what we were supposed to be doing today as it's all gone blank. I should add that to the 'grateful' list!*
- I will walk Reggie every day – *I didn't walk him today, but only because Mum was home early and I went straight to taekwondo. I've spent time cuddling him this evening, which has made me feel loads better.*

Success

- I didn't cry, and I looked after myself today.

- I went to taekwondo even though I was tempted to come straight home.

Gratitude

- I am grateful that Reggie has let me give him cuddles this evening. Sometimes he wanders off and lies down somewhere else but tonight, he stayed close by me. He knows me so well.

Forty-five

After yesterday, I wasn't feeling the love for heading back to Sixth Form. I had to go back to the dreaded classroom with those idiots, Matt and Adam, being their macho selves again. It's not long until we've got exams so I have been doing my best to concentrate but I found it hard today. Luckily, I didn't have to work with them again, but listening to them chatting all the way through class was more distracting than usual. It was like I was automatically listening out for them to say something that would freak me out, like I was on high alert. Frankie didn't help by counting down the days until our exam and that did make me freak out a bit. At least I was distracted for a few minutes while I panicked about how much revision I needed to do.

'Maybe you'll have to miss some taekwondo so you can get all this revision done,' Frankie had said, when I had finished explaining how worried I was about the exams.

'Are you joking? That's the only thing keeping me sane,' I shrieked.

'Whoa, I'd question the claim on sanity, do you know how high-pitched you're getting,' she argued.

Fair point. There was no way I was going to miss training. I know that going down that route doesn't help me all. I'll figure out a way of getting it all done. If those two idiots can still be in Sixth Form, I can pass these exams.

They didn't say anything that freaked me out today though and both even said 'See ya,' as they left the room and we headed in opposite directions for the next class. They seriously had no idea at all about the impact their words had. That shouldn't come as I surprise to me I guess, it's not the first time I've been hurt by someone else's words and they either didn't notice or didn't care. This time, at least they weren't deliberately trying to hurt me. I wonder if they'd be bothered if they knew?

'You're on another planet today,' said Frankie.

We were heading off to separate classes. I was meeting Maya as we had Psychology and just said, 'Sorry, I'll text you later.'

Frankie wandered off. I watched as she walked away, hoping that I hadn't annoyed her. Luckily for me, she's pretty laid back. The opposite to me. We make a good team.

Maya walked over. 'Why are you staring at her?' she asked.

'I'm not, I'm thinking,' I quickly replied. I wasn't sure what else to say. Had I been staring? I don't think I had. I quickly changed the subject. 'Have you done that assignment?'

I then had another panic about the exams as Maya and I talked about how much we didn't know. The more we talked, the more we realised we didn't know anything. There's no way I'm going to fail these exams; I don't care what it takes.

I'm supposed to be writing an essay about memory for Psychology at the moment. We had a choice of questions that we could answer and I stupidly agreed to work on one about reconstructive memory, because Maya said it would be the most interesting. To be fair, it is interesting, but it's making me think too. We have to talk about eyewitness testimonies and how reliable they are when different words are used to ask the witness about specific events.

'Can you imagine being an eyewitness and someone being sent to prison because of what you've said?' Maya questioned.

I can't escape my brain at the moment as the simplest word or question takes me back to thinking about what happened. I'm feeling okay and definitely keeping my head together, but I wonder if they'll ever come a time where I can think about questions like that without it feeling so personal, or whether I can say something out loud and speak from experience. I'm not sure.

I need to get the essay done, so at the moment, I just have to focus. We're writing the essay on car crashes, so as long as Maya doesn't come up with any more deep and meaningful questions, I should be okay.

I'm trying to plan my revision schedule. One thing I'm really good at is the planning. I learnt that from my GCSEs. So far, I have an amazing, neatly drawn out, colour-coded plan. I was about to actually open a book when I had a text from Frankie asking if I was free in a couple of weeks to go with her to a party. It's a party for her army friend, whom I've never met, but heard a lot about.

'Just u & me, a wkend away x,' she replied when I said I'd love to go with her.

I feel nervous and excited but I'm not sure why.

I need to open a book so I think, *I'm not going to get anywhere while I only have my plan. Even if it is a really colourful plan!*

First of all:

Goals

- It's August and I have my next belt in taekwondo – *It's all good, training sessions are in my plan and obviously, colour coded as red.*
- It's half term and I have handed in all of my assignments.
- I have stuck to my revision plan every day.

Success

- I have started to get sorted to make sure I do my revision.
- Today, I have been to Sixth Form, walked Reggie twice, done my homework, planned my revision AND I'm about to get started. That's pretty good, right?

Gratitude

- I am grateful that the sun was shining for both walks with Reggie

- I'm excited and grateful that Frankie has asked me to this party, I'll need to check with Mum that she can give me a lift, but I'm sure she'll be happy to get rid of me for a night.

Forty-six

It's been a weird day and an even weirder evening.

I had lunch with Maya and Katie today, which was nice and almost like old times. We sent Callie a selfie telling her we missed her and got the reply, 'Love ya loserz x.' This made us miss her more. I bet she doesn't care about exams.

'No Frankie today?' asked Katie. 'You two are joined at the hip these days.'

What did she mean by that? It's hardly like her and her boyfriend, Cal. I'm sure the only reason she was having lunch with us was because he'd got something better to do than spend yet another lunch break with her.

'She went home. I don't think she's got classes this afternoon.'

I don't 'think', I know. I know her timetable better than my own. I don't know why I felt so self-conscious though. I'm sure I saw Katie and Maya smile at each other as if they'd been talking about me. Why would they be talking about me? It's the same sort of smile that Frankie gives me when Katie starts talking about her boyfriend, Cal. Why would they be saying anything that would make them smile like that?

I tried to forget about it while we talked about revision, and what we were worrying about with each of our subjects. I couldn't forget about it though. For the first time since leaving secondary school, I felt paranoid as if I was being talked about behind my back. This was different and even more frightening because they were my friends, not the evil bullies who hated me from the moment they saw me. These two were supposed to like me and I was supposed to be able to trust them.

I was distracted from thinking about it this evening, with something else that was quite weird. Sammy came over for dinner and was asking me what I wanted to do when I left Sixth Form. 'I have to pass my exams first,' I said.

'Well, if you pass your exams, what do you want to do?' he asked.

I liked that he didn't say what most people say, which is, 'Of course you'll pass' or 'You'll be fine.' They have no idea if I'm going pass or if I'll be fine. I might fail and have a complete breakdown; they don't know. Anyway, I told him that I still didn't know what I wanted to do. But that wasn't good enough.

Sammy was turning into a career advisor. He asked if I had thought about working with dogs.

'No, never,' I replied.

'Reggie certainly responds really well to you,' he said, which I thought was kind of nice.

'Which of your subjects to you like the most?' He really wasn't giving up.

I thought about it and I couldn't decide between Sport and Psychology. 'I'm not sure if I really like learning all about sport, or if it's just that I love taekwondo,' I admitted. In reality, I wasn't sure if I liked sport because I had the most fun in those lessons, most of the time.

'There are a lot of people making a really good living out of Sport Psychology.'

Where did he get those things from? I was finding it hard not to like him when he came out with stuff like that.

'You could be the psychologist for the Olympic Taekwondo Team,' he suggested

Hold on a minute, I thought. 'Is that an actual job?' My head was spinning.

'Sure, I was reading about it on the interweb.'

'Interweb, who says that?' I replied. Mum glared at me. 'Sorry, I just didn't know that was an actual job.'

Sammy was looking very pleased with himself and then wouldn't shut up about it, but I have to say, he was making a lot of sense. 'Sports Psychologists help the athletes to be the best they can be,' he continued.

'I thought that was the coach's job,' I said, trying to figure out how it would work.

'It is; they make sure the athlete has all the skills and they work hard together to get all of the practical elements right. Then, the psychologist works on their head! They help them with motivation, visualisation and managing pressure at big events.'

Okay, so this does sounds too good to be true.

'It's like what you're doing with Amie.'

Sorry, but how exactly is it anything like that? The look on my face must have said it all.

He understood my surprise. 'Seriously, you're not taking her to school or doing any work with her. You're talking to her. Helping to motivate her to help herself.'

Where did he get this stuff from? He was turning into a male Jane and he was making me like him.

'You've created a safe environment for her. Taking Reggie means that she's relaxed and can enjoy herself without pressure, which means she's much more likely to make positive decisions. You could take Reggie to the Olympics and watch everyone relax and then win medals.'

O.M.G.

'Sammy, you've done something incredible.' Mum's voice broke through the following silence. 'Dani's lost for words, and that never happens.'

'Reggie at the Olympics,' was all I could say. 'Could you imagine?' I had visions of him racing after javelins, jumping in the pool and thinking that the tennis matches for just for his benefit. Tennis balls are the best thing ever in his world.

'Can I go upstairs?' I said. With a nod from Mum I raced away from the table. I needed to get to my laptop. I needed to find out everything about this and if it was even possible. I hadn't felt this excited in ages, this positive, this focused.

'Thank you, Sammy,' I remembered to say before I made the leap onto the stairs.

He nodded, smiling, while I could see Mum was beaming from ear to ear.

Okay, I admit, I could get to really like this guy. A 'Sports Psychologist'. Who knew?

Forty-seven

I have been totally buzzing about this whole Sports Psychologist thing. I've been so focused I didn't mind at all when Frankie sent a message to say the party had been cancelled. I had been looking forward to it, but I had also found out that there are actual degrees in Sport Psychology. They sound amazing. One description I read said that I'd be learning about mental toughness, self-confidence, motivation, stress and anxiety. How amazing would it be to learn about these in relation to sport and helping people be the best they can be, rather than remembering the rubbish times when I think about these things.

If I think about mental toughness, I think about trying to get myself out of the dark places. If I think about self-confidence, it immediately makes me think about how mine was destroyed. Weirdly though, my first thought wasn't about the rape. It was about the bullies. I definitely wasn't a ray of sunshine when I started that school, but those bitches destroyed any tiny bit of confidence I had left. If I think about motivation, I remember Jane telling me that I could motivate myself to get out of bed, get up and get showered. That was a massive achievement for me not so long ago! If I think about stress and anxiety, well, the list is quite long of things I could describe, and none of them make me feel good.

What if all of those things had a different focus? They could be the reason for focusing on good stuff. What could be better than focusing on being brilliant at sport? I feel stressed and anxious before I do one of my gradings, but it's not a bad feeling, it shows me how important it is to me. That's a really different feeling to when I look back at the other times I felt stressed and anxious. I know that I'm not an Olympic athlete in the making, and that's okay because my goal is to get my black belt, not to go to the Olympics. When I'm training, everything is okay. I'm focused and motivated. When I leave a training session, I feel as if I can do anything. The weird thing is, it's those same words that have also made me think about the worst times in my life.

I saw Amie today and it was perfect timing. I told her that Sammy thinks that having Reggie around helps us both relax and make better decisions.

'Oh, so you like him now?' she said.

'He's okay, I guess,' was all I'd admit to.

'He's right, when Reggie's with us everything is loads more fun.'

Fun. Maybe that's the key. Sport is fun and those words mean different things in the world of sport.

'You know when you're teaching Reggie a new trick or something, he's having fun, so he remembers it and then does it again when you ask him,' Amie said. 'I suppose it's like that for us, we have fun with him, so when we talk and decide we're going to do something, we're more likely to do it.'

Is everyone turning into Jane?

'Everyone should have a Reggie,' were Amie's next words of wisdom.

Maybe she's right. Maybe Reggie is the secret to success. Watching him dancing around with his ball, trying to get a small dog to play with him, I wasn't convinced! He made us laugh though. He made the day fun.

'I've got some homework that I need your help with,' Amie said, looking at the floor and almost apologising.

'Why are you saying it like that?'

'It's for a business project. I was going to look at maybe planning to write that book we talked about, only if that's okay, and only if you don't mind.'

I felt jealous. I am really ashamed, but I felt jealous.

Amie broke the silence. 'I won't do it if you're not okay with it, I want us to do it together but I thought it would be a good project. I know that it's our thing and I won't do it unless you're sure.'

'I think it's a great idea,' I managed to say.

It was a great idea. It was not like I'd done anything about it. I remember that it was Jane's idea to start with. I was telling her how much I had enjoyed being able to help Amie and that it would be amazing to be able to help more people. It was then that she joked about writing a book. A few days later, I was with Amie and our mums, walking Reggie in the park. It was the first time Amie had met Reggie and we were having a brilliant day. Amie had recently got out of hospital and she had inspired me that day.

Amie is one of the most inspirational people I know, so I quickly realised that actually, I should be grateful that she wants me to be involved. It wasn't even my idea to start with!

'Sorry, it just took me by surprise, I haven't thought about that in ages,' I said. 'You should definitely work on this and if you can figure out a way to make us our millions that would be awesome.'

I could see the relief on Amie's face and the feeling of jealousy turned in to a feeling of awe and excitement.

Amie has so much courage and considering that it's usually she who's helping me, I know that she could help so many more people too. 'What's the plan then?'

Amie then went into overdrive. She had obviously given it a lot of thought and said that she wanted people to know that there was life after rape. Life could be amazing and there was no reason why things had to be rubbish. 'You taught me that, which is why we have to write this together,' she said.

'I would be honoured to work with you on this, thanks for asking me.'

That was the truth. Never mind goals and success.

Today is all about being grateful for Amie. She didn't have to include me and she didn't have to say those words. I wish that neither of us needed to write this book, but the fact that we're still here, doing well and being able to write it, can only be a good thing.

Forty-eight

Finally, half term is here. I'm supposed to be revising and sticking to my colourful and well-planned-out revision timetable. Instead, I have spent the last hour choosing a new colour for my bedroom. Mum said that I could decorate my room in the summer but she started decorating downstairs yesterday and I got overexcited with the thought of a new room. Well, not a new room, but it will feel that way.

Sammy was helping with the decorating and I could hear him and Mum laughing a lot.

'I'm supposed to be revising and you're not helping,' I said when I went downstairs to make yet another drink. 'Why is Reggie blue? I'm going to have to bath him.'

'Oh no you're not. That sounds like another way of avoiding revision to me,' said Mum.

Sammy promised he'd return Reggie to his natural colour before he went home. 'He ran off with a paintbrush when I went to the loo,' he admitted. 'And then he bounced around the garden with it, splashing paint on himself in the process.'

I was sure that was funny to watch.

'Fancy joining us for dinner,' asked Sammy. 'My treat.'

Before I could answer Mum said, 'Only if you spend the rest of the day revising, then you can join us for a break from all the studying.'

'Sure, dinner sounds great,' I said to Sammy. I thought revising was probably a better idea than choosing paint colours, even though it wasn't as much fun. If I wanted to take Reggie to the Olympics, then I had to pass my exams!

Revision is so boring. Seriously boring. I would actually rather have been downstairs, painting. Mum and Sammy did make an effort to be quiet and I was as productive as I could be, but my mind kept wandering. One minute I was thinking about being at uni and then next I was thinking about writing this book with Amie. How do you even start writing a book? No doubt Amie will come up with a brilliant plan for us now she's become a business mastermind. Then, what about uni? I am excited about the idea of Sport Psychology, but I'm not so sure about leaving home, and by 'home', I mean Reggie. I don't have to worry about that for a while though and if I don't pass my exams, I won't have to worry about it at all.

Mum brought my lunch up to my room and said, 'I know that you're working really hard and I'm proud of you, but it's okay to take breaks too, come downstairs whenever you want.'

Luckily, she didn't see that I was actually messaging Frankie on my laptop and not revising at all. Oops!

Frankie is not helping with revision. She sends me YouTube links of new music videos that I 'have to watch'. Then, we start talking about what we like or don't like about the video, watch more videos and before I know it, I'm an hour behind on my revision plan.

'You'll be fine,' she keeps saying.

What if I'm not fine? What if I fail and have to do this whole year all over again?

'Piss off. I'm going to do some work. Talk to you later.' I have to send the message to get rid of her. I don't want to get rid of her, but if I don't learn something, I'm going to get more freaked out and then I won't learn anything at all. As soon as I start to freak out and panic, my brain decides it won't remember anything at all.

I've done okay with my coursework and I know that the exams are only a small part of the grade, but they could still mean I fail. If I totally mess up the exams, I'm screwed. I'm feeling more motivated to pass now that I know I have to get good grades to get on a Sport Psychology course. I still haven't decided if that's definitely what I want to do, but it does make a lot of sense.

Dinner was great this evening, mainly because I got presents! Sammy had bought me two books.

'I know that you have enough to read at the moment with all your revision,' he said, 'but I thought these might be useful and help you have fun in the process.'

Fun, there it is again, I need to have more fun! One was a book by a famous runner who says that her talent in running meant nothing until she changed her mindset. The other was a book on trick training for dogs. Awesome!

Sammy smiled. 'I know that you and Reggie want to win the tricks category at the dog show, so maybe it's about skills and mindset.'

Definitely, Reggie has the skills, I just don't know how to bring out the best in him.

I smiled back. 'I've been thinking about what you said and it does make a lot of sense. I like the idea of being able to help people motivate themselves.'

Sammy looked pleased and said that he was glad he finally said something useful.

'Thank you for the books too,' I said. 'They look a lot more interesting than the ones I have to read for Sixth Form.'

He laughed as Mum made it very clear that the books were for after a day of revision to help me relax, and not as an alternative to revision. Both Sammy and I were then told off for rolling our eyes.

I started reading the book about the runner when I got home. It's amazing. She is amazing. She was winning races and was the fastest runner her country had ever seen, but she was so frightened of failing that she started to sabotage her own success. When I told Mum, she said that I'd be sabotaging my own success if I didn't do everything possible to pass my exams. I wanted to roll my eyes, but she had a point.

Forty-nine

I'll never admit to this, but I've had way too much fun at the charity dog show today. I'm writing this having just got home from an amazing 'End of Half Term' party, organised by someone Frankie knows from another class.

'Please come,' she said as she called to invite me. 'It makes up for the one that was cancelled.'

I had the best time, but I'm still more excited about the dog show.

Reggie came second in the trick competition. Oh yes, we're getting better. Mum was gushing with pride and Sammy came along to support us too. He seemed impressed with our performance. 'If it wasn't for the book you gave me, I'd never have been able to teach Reggie those tricks,' I admitted.

I was quite nervous. It was the first time that Sammy had come with us to something like this. We've been out for meals, and I know that he takes Reggie out for walks with Mum quite often, but we've never done something like this. Reggie was beyond excited when we all got into the car and he realised that he had all of his favourite people in one place. Sammy is actually good with Reggie and I think Reggie enjoys having him around. I should listen to what Reggie is telling me, as he's a good judge of character.

I didn't enter Reggie into any of the other categories, as last time he was quite tired by the time he got to the trick competition. I wanted him to be alert and at his best! There was a strong chance that I was taking this way too seriously.

He was amazing. We'd been practicing and he did me proud. The only slight blip was when the judge came to present him with his rosette and he tried to eat it. We pinned it to his harness, out of reach and then he became much more interested in the bag of toys and treats I'd been given on his behalf. The rosette was no longer of any interest whatsoever as he stuck his head in the bag and came out with a squeaky ball.

'He can never be accused of being a scary dog,' said the judge, laughing at Reggie who was making the most of his moment in the spotlight.

'Never,' I replied.

As we walked out of the ring, with Reggie now annoying the other dogs with his squeaking, we saw a woman running towards us through the crowd. Before I realised who it was, Reggie dropped his ball and pulled me towards her. She knelt down to greet him and his tail was wagging so fast I'm definitely going to have bruises.

'Oh wow, Bev, hello,' Mum squealed as everyone was getting way too excited.

I then realised who it was that my boy was covering in slobbery kisses. Bev was the lady from the rescue centre who had looked after Reggie. She had helped us, teaching us everything we needed to know about him. She cried when we took him home. She had grown very attached to him and said that if it wasn't for her own house full of dogs, she'd have taken him home herself.

I couldn't believe that Reggie remembered her. There was absolutely no doubt that he knew exactly who Bev was and he made it clear that he was ecstatic to see her. I didn't know that dogs had that ability.

Bev was crying, at least, I think they were tears and not just Reggie's slobber as she told us, 'It's the best feeling in the world when I see one of the rescue dogs doing so well with their new family.'

Now, I know that Reggie loves me and I know that he loves Mum and maybe Sammy, but today when we were all sitting together and catching up, he chose to go and lie next to Bev. He leaned in to her as she stroked him and looked at her with such adoration as she was telling him how happy she was for him. It was as if he was thanking her and letting her know that he was doing just fine. Sammy offered to take a picture of us so that Bev could share the success story for other people who were looking to rescue a dog.

'No, we'll get someone else to take it, Reggie would want you in the picture too,' I said. I guess that was our first 'family' photograph.

I left Reggie snoring on the sofa, using his new squeaky ball as a pillow and went to the party. I didn't want to tell anyone about the show as I already think I talk about Reggie too much, but I spent most of the evening with Frankie and told her about our second place.

'Don't tell Reggie, but second place is first loser,' was her way of saying 'congratulations'. 'That's really cool,' she added. 'So am I right in thinking you keep telling me to piss off because you're playing with Reggie and not because you're revising?'

'I'm doing both,' I said.

She didn't look too impressed but started telling me about her visit to see her army friend and I was soon forgiven.

I had a laugh tonight, I felt like I was part of something. There were lots of people I recognised but had never spoken to and it didn't matter. Most people were dancing and having a drink while Frankie and I chilled out and chatted. Maya joined us for a while but said we were way too boring and the last I saw of her she was dancing with some guy I'd never seen before. Needless to say, Katie and her boyfriend, Cal, were inseparable.

Today has been a really good day but it's back to reality soon, with exams to get through. Taekwondo and Reggie will keep me sane and I definitely need to make more time to see Frankie as I always have a good time when I'm with her.

Fifty

I haven't written in here much for the last couple of weeks. It's been so busy now that the exams are only days away but not much has actually happened. It has been a constant cycle of walkies, Sixth Form, revision, walkies, taekwondo, more revision. Mum started to take Reggie out for me in the mornings but I found that I felt worse and couldn't concentrate as much when I didn't take him. Getting up and having a laugh with Reggie switches my brain on. Mum wasn't going to argue with that.

I saw Amie yesterday and she has really got into this book writing project. They have to hand it in as part of their coursework so I've promised her that I'll make some time to see her in the next week.

'It's not like we actually have to write it yet,' she said. 'We just have to decide what we're going to do so I can write the business plan.'

She sounded like she really knew what she was talking about, and when I left her house, I honestly believed that we could make it happen. I felt excited about it, but I know what I'm like and I'm easily distracted from revision so I'm doing my best not to think about it too much.

I had a 'miss u' text from Frankie this morning and I realised I had been really rubbish at making time to see her.

It's weird because I really want to see her but I'm almost nervous about picking up the phone to text her and arrange something. 'What if she's sick of me?' or 'What if she thinks I'm a loser?' are questions that go around my head when I haven't heard from her for a couple of days. Then, she'll send me a message and the fears go away for a little while.

I replied and asked her if she was free over the weekend. We're going to go into town and 'revise' over a pizza. Mum said that she would only give me a lift if she saw that I was taking revision books with me. Deal. That'll be a good distraction just before the exams start.

Taekwondo is going well and I'm working hard for my next belt. On training days, I come home and I'm buzzing, so I make the most of it and get some revision done too. I'm definitely feeling focused and am sticking to the revision timetable as much as I can. I'm just not sure if it's going to be enough. It's been a tough year, with ups and downs, so I don't know if I've missed too much to be able to catch up now. I'm trying though.

'Yes, you're very trying,' is what my comedy genius mother comes back with when I say that.

Jane called to ask how revision was going and to check I was looking after myself. I think she was impressed with how I'd been sticking to the plan, and said that she didn't mind that I was using Jaffa Cakes, my comfort eating food, as my revision snacks as long as I was exercising and sticking to my plan.

Jaffa Cakes are usually a sign that I'm heading to the dark place and I'm in need of comfort and distraction. I hadn't thought about it, but I'd been feeling great and working hard, enjoying them as a snack. Jane said that this was progress and its things like this that show just how far I've come.

That woman really can find a message in anything, even biscuits. I told her that I'd been finding out about Sport Psychology. 'The sounds perfect,' she said, sounding almost as excited as I was when I first started researching it. 'A friend of mine from uni is a Sport Psychologist so if you want, I could see if you could do some work experience over the summer.'

I have never been more excited about the thought of 'working' over the summer.

'Exams first, and then I'll see what I can arrange,' Jane said. A clear instruction that I wouldn't be getting any more information about that until after the dreaded exams. It's as if she knows how easily distracted I am.

I've had a bit of a think about my goals, especially now that I'm feeling so motivated. Things are going well for me right now, and Jane always says that's when I mustn't forget to write in this journal.

Goals

- It's August and I have my next belt in taekwondo – *My red colour coding on my timetable is probably the only thing I've stuck to. I'm training hard and loving it.*
- I have handed in all of my assignments on time, ready to focus on the exams. *Yes! I handed in the last one yesterday and it was an amazing feeling, until I remembered that I still had to pass the exams!*
- I have stuck to my revision plan every day. *Almost every day. That counts.*
- I will walk into every exam knowing I am prepared. *To do this, I have to stick to the plan and I'm doing my best. I'm feeling more prepared, but still have a lot to read.*

Success

- I am proud of myself for finishing all of my assignments and I was pleased with what I'd written, and that hasn't happened for a while.
- I've been making decisions that mean I feel better and I'm not taking the easy option. So, like when Mum offered to do the morning walkies and I could have stayed in bed, I knew that going out with Reggie would make me feel better.

Gratitude

- I am grateful that Amie has asked me to be part of her project. I'm excited about it.
- I'm grateful that things are going well, that there aren't any dramas and that life is good at the moment. It has been a

while since I've felt like things are relaxed and I've been able to just be a teenager.

Fifty-one

I hate exams. I hate exams more than I hate revision. I really hate revision.

Today's exam was so hard. English is not fun at all.

Because I felt like my whole brain had been drained, I cancelled on Amie and went into town with Frankie and Maya. I just needed to be around people who understood how horrible this whole exam situation had been. I sent her a message saying how sorry I was, and that I desperately needed to revise for my next exam. She replied saying, 'I bet you're with Frankie, not revising.'

What was she on about? Did I talk about Frankie a lot? I didn't think I talked about her that much? I didn't reply because there was no way I was going to lie to Amie, even though the first message was a bit of lie I guess. I felt bad enough without having to explain myself to her.

I want to help her and I really want to work on the book with her, but my head is so focused on the exams and I don't really want to talk about what we have to talk about.

At the moment, I am really enjoying being happy. That probably sounds stupid considering I'm in the middle of exam hell, but I'm worried about normal stuff. This time last year, I was going through exam hell and it was far from normal. I'm worried that if I start going through all the plans with Amie and we talk about what's going in the book and how we can help other people through talking about our experiences, my brain will go back to thinking about what happened. If it does do that, I won't be able to concentrate on the exams. I have to concentrate on the exams. I'll sort things out with Amie and sort out another date, I shouldn't have arranged something for today as I knew that I'd be knackered after English.

We had a laugh in town. It was the perfect way to forget about the exam and I laughed a lot. As I started to relax, I could think about the exam in a different way. Maya had taken English too and as we talked about what we'd written, I realised that I'd actually done okay. Maya is amazing at English and when I told her some of things I'd put in my answers, she said she wished she had thought of that.

'Are you kidding?' I asked, as it was usually Maya who was helping me with the answers.

'Seriously, it sounds like you nailed it,' she said when I told her about my final essay.

She made me feel a whole lot better and I really hope she's right. I desperately hope I've 'nailed it'.

Frankie burst the bubble by saying, 'You need to do the same thing tomorrow, for the PE exam.'

Tomorrow? Argh, I needed to get home to swallow my PE books before yet another day of hell.

Mum came to pick me up and she had Reggie in the car who looked as bad as he smelt. 'Don't ask,' Mum said as I got in the car. 'I'll bath him when we get home.'

Reggie had obviously had a fun walk, even if Mum hadn't! I was not sorry I'd missed that walk.

'I'll make dinner while you get on with your revision,' she added, and she ushered Reggie into the garden.

'Thanks, I need brain food,' I said. She laughed and told me that she could only promise 'food'.

Before I attempted to read about sporty type things, I messaged Amie:

Hey, I'm really sorry about 2day. The exam was soooooo hard and I have another 1 tomo. I shouldn't have promised to come over 2day, my fault. I do really want to work on this with you. I feel bad about letting u down. Are u free this wkend? I don't have exams until Wed next wk. Pls? x

Amie messaged straight back saying that it was okay, I had to pass my exams and that her mum would sort the weekend out with my mum. I reckoned that was because she wanted a day out with Reggie. I couldn't blame her.

I feel better now I've said 'sorry' and that we have another date to meet up.

I'm sitting here writing this. I should be revising. My brain is empty. There should be loads of room now that I've got rid of all the 'English' information, but I'm just so tired. I tried reading through my notes and the words just don't make any sense. I think I need to have some Reggie time, have dinner and then try again before I go to bed. I might wait until Mum has bathed him because he did not smell good at all. I have just put a huge 'tick' through today's exam on my timetable and that felt good. One down.

Goals

- It's August and I have my next belt in taekwondo – *I'll be training after tomorrow's exam, I reckon I'll need to hit things afterwards!*
- I have stuck to my revision plan every day. *Today is a bit of a fail, but I'll do some reading after dinner.*
- I will walk into every exam knowing I am prepared. *I did actually feel okay this morning, and even though I'm not reading at the moment, I have already done loads of revision for tomorrow.*

Success

- I wrote lots of words in today's exam. Considering it's an English exam, I'm taking that as a success.

Gratitude

- I am grateful that Amie has forgiven me for today. I'll make it up to her and be extra helpful this weekend.

- I'm grateful to Maya for making me feel loads better about today's exam. I actually think I might have done okay, which is a good feeling.
- I'm grateful that I had a fun afternoon and that I'm not too freaked out about tomorrow.

Fifty-two

That's it. No more exams. Today has been horrible and amazing. It started out okay, was then horrible thanks to the most difficult exam EVER, and then was amazing thanks to the best taekwondo session EVER.

I'd been feeling okay about the exams; I was as prepared as I could have been. There's always more I could have done, but I did my best. I stuck to the revision timetable as much as I could have and I did go into each exam feeling prepared. Nervous, but prepared.

This morning was just crazy. Looking around the room, I wasn't the only one who was wondering if they were in the right exam. I didn't really have to worry about the answers because I was too busy worrying about making sense of the questions. Any dream I had of finishing the exams on a high was shattered as soon as I opened the paper.

Until today, I'd only worried about whether I'd answered the questions properly, how much I had missed or whether I could have added more. Today, I left wondering if my answer made any sense at all because I didn't understand the question in the first place. I just wrote down everything I knew, in the hope that someone would give me some marks. The only thing that made me feel better was that everyone else did the same thing.

'Nufink u can do 'bout it now, dude. It's summer holibobs 4 u! x,' was Frankie's reply when I told her how horrible it had been.

She's right, no more Sixth Form for the summer. We can come and get our results to make sure that we're allowed back in September, but that's it. Finished. No more revision. No more exams. Not for me anyway. Frankie has her last exam tomorrow and we're all going out for the day to celebrate surviving exam hell.

Back in my room, I put the biggest 'tick' through today's

exam. The final thing on my timetable. Then, I took it off the wall, screwed it up into a ball and Reggie and I played football with it in the garden until it was completely destroyed. That felt soooooooo good. All I wanted to do was lie down and watch the TV. It felt surreal, not having anything to do. I was knackered and started to talk myself out of going to taekwondo.

I'm so glad I dragged my tired arse to the session. In the panic about the exam, I'd forgotten that we had a guest trainer coming. Steph is one of the most successful female taekwondo players in the UK and within seconds, I wasn't feeling tired any more. I was feeling more motivated than ever.

She was like Jane on speed, with the taekwondo skills to match her amazingly positive attitude. Just being in the same room as her made me feel like I could achieve everything I ever dreamed of, and then some. Not only was she a sporting champion, she was an engineer, succeeding in a male dominated world, a mum of two small humans and three big canines. She made me laugh because she talked about her dogs more than she talked about her children.

She talked to us about how she had used taekwondo to help her through the difficult times and how it had kept her sane. She didn't tell us what the difficult times were, and it didn't matter. We all have different stuff to deal with and everyone in the room knew that taekwondo was the best way to get some focus back.

'If you're struggling with who you are, if you are coming to terms with your past and how it can inspire and not dictate your future, sport will give you the strength to be who you are supposed to be,' she said wisely.

I think every single one of us felt that she was talking directly to us. There was silence and I wasn't the only one who wiped away a tear. She was talking to me.

At that moment, I knew. I knew that I had been struggling with whom I am now.

Steph gently broke through the silence and told us to go and get changed so that she could take us through one of her training sessions. I've never felt pain like it, yet it felt so good at the same time. Steph showed me that I was capable of more than I ever thought possible.

'What would you love to be able to do?' she asked.

I was embarrassed as I told her, 'I dream of wearing a black belt.'

'Say it with pride,' she said. 'You're not far away from your black belt; it's well within your reach.'

I thought about the book that Sammy had given me, about the runner who sabotaged her own success. I have nothing to be embarrassed about because I want to achieve something. I have nothing to be embarrassed about at all.

'Whatever you have to say, say it with pride,' Steph whispered before moving on to the next person. I wiped away another tear.

Goals

- It's August and I am wearing my new belt with pride. *Not long now and I'll be ready for my grading.*
- In the summer holiday, I'll spend some time with Jane's friend, learning about what a Sport Psychologist really does. *I'm excited about this, Jane said that she's sorting out some dates for me to go and 'work'!*

Success

- I have finished all of my exams for my first year at Sixth Form, handed in all of my coursework and despite a few meltdowns along the way, I hope I've done okay.

Gratitude

- It's pretty obvious, but Steph coming to our session today has been the most amazing thing that has happened to me in a while. I'm grateful to her for spending time with us, and for spending time with me. Her words meant so much and I'm feeling stronger than ever.

Fifty-three

Just as I thought things couldn't get any better, today happened.

My first day of holiday freedom started with the sun shining and a long walk with my main man. We were honoured to be joined by Katie and Bailey and we had the best morning. Reggie and Bailey were excited to see each other and raced around the park for an hour while Katie and I caught up, properly. We talked about everything and nothing, it was like old times and she apologised for being so focused on Cal (she didn't say, her boyfriend, which was weird) and said she missed hanging out with us all.

'Well, today is the perfect day to start again,' I said, as we had a day in town planned to celebrate the end of exams. 'Just us, like old times.'

'Well, sort of.' She laughed. 'I'm guessing Frankie will be there?'

'Well, she hasn't ditched me for a boyfriend,' I said.

Katie screwed up her face and replied. 'Like that would happen.'

At that moment, we heard a splash and, as usual, the boys had found their way to the pond and continued to play in the water, making a lot of noise and entertaining all the people who had stopped to watch them.

'We really should remember to bring towels,' Katie said, after we were both soaked by their signature shake offs. 'Right, let's get these guys home, dried off and then we can go out.'

Having done just that, I headed into town to meet up with everyone. Mum had already agreed to walk Reggie later on and pick me up whenever I was ready. 'Within reason, obviously. Have fun and stay safe,' she shouted as she left this morning, late for work as usual.

I felt different as I left the house, locked the door and started walking. Free. I felt free. I don't know whether it was because the exams had finished, the holiday had started or the amazing session with Steph, but it felt incredible.

'Where shall we start?' shouted Callie. We had all gathered outside the shopping centre.

'Pizza,' was the answer and we headed to our favourite place, already sure what we were going to order because we knew the menu inside out.

Finding a corner table, we were ready to start celebrating.

'What are these 'exams' you speak of,' Callie joked. Being at art college meant that she had loads of coursework but escaped the exam hell. While we were sharing stories of impossible questions, and the realisation that we'd written something really stupid or missed the point of the question, she sat back and laughed at us. 'Listening to you lot makes me one hundred per cent sure I made the right decision.'

I don't think I have ever enjoyed pizza as much as I did this afternoon. Everyone was getting on brilliantly, as if we'd never been apart and Frankie had always been a part of the group. Her and Callie are like a comedy double act, both trying to be more outrageous than the other. They had us in stitches for the whole afternoon.

'Who needs a comedy film when we've got you two?' asked Maya.

We had decided that we'd go to the cinema for a laugh and that was Maya's way of telling us to hurry up because the film would be starting soon. She doesn't like to be late because she'll miss the trailers.

The laughter continued on the way to the cinema with Callie taking selfies with random strangers 'in the name of art', whatever that means and Frankie trying to photobomb at every opportunity. Katie looked embarrassed but couldn't help laughing as Callie then tripped up and fell at the feet of a guy they both agreed was seriously good-looking.

There wasn't a queue for the film, which made Maya very happy.

'It probably means the film is crap,' shouted Callie, which didn't impress the guy selling us our tickets.

'Popcorn or pick 'n' mix?' I asked Frankie as we both headed for the shop.

'We could get one of each and share?'

I'm not someone who usually wants to share popcorn but, somehow, it seemed like a genius idea. 'No liquorice though,' I said when Frankie started to fill a bag with sweets.

'Obviously,' she replied. 'Who would eat that?'

The lights were dimming and I could see a few people looking unimpressed as we walked in, still laughing. We found a row of empty seats near the back and Frankie made her way in first. I followed, sat down, and finally we were all quiet. Much to the relief of everyone around us.

'Shhhh,' came a voice from behind us as Callie decided she needed to open her giant bag of sweets, which catapulted into the air and made us all laugh again.

As the film started, I don't think I'd ever felt happier. I was out with the most amazing group of friends. I felt incredibly lucky. I had no idea that things were about to get even better.

'You know I like you, right?' whispered Frankie as we were sitting, sharing the armrest and both reaching into the tub of popcorn.

'Yeah, I know. You know I like you too, right?'

LODESTONE BOOKS

Lodestone Books
YOUNG ADULT FICTION

Lodestone Books is a new imprint, which offers a broad spectrum of subjects in YA/NA literature. Compelling reading, the Teen/Young/New Adult reader is sure to find something edgy, enticing and innovative. From dystopian societies, through a whole range of fantasy, horror, science fiction and paranormal fiction, all the way to the other end of the phere, historical drama, steam-punk adventure, and everything in between (including crime, coming of age and contemporary romance). Whatever your preference you will discover it here.
If you have enjoyed this book, why not tell other readers by posting a review on your preferred book site. Recent bestsellers from Lodestone Books are:

AlphaNumeric

Nicolas Forzy

When dyslexic teenager Stu accidentally transports himself into a world populated by living numbers and letters, his arrival triggers a prophecy that pulls two rival communities into war.
Paperback: 978-1-78279-506-3 ebook: 978-1-78279-505-6

Shanti and the Magic Mandala

F.T. Camargo

In this award-winning YA novel, six teenagers from around the world gather for a frantic chase across Peru, in search of a